W9-BTA-238

Mason had envisioned Norah as a woman in her sixties who would provide a grandmotherly model for the children in the therapeutic program.

But Norah wasn't grandmotherly. He could hardly believe she was forty-two. Her straight, silvery-gray hair was arranged over her forehead in a wispy mist, then flowed in soft layers to the base of her neck. Her bright, clear blue eyes were highlighted by long black lashes that contrasted with her ivory skin.

Mason had been lonely since his father's death, but he hadn't understood how lonely until Norah had entered his home. Yearnings that Mason thought he'd stifled forever suddenly seemed important again....

Books by Irene Brand

Love Inspired

IRENE BRAND

Writing has been a lifelong interest of this author, who says that she started her first novel when she was eleven years old and hasn't finished it yet. However, since 1984, she's published twenty-four contemporary and historical novels and three nonfiction titles with publishers such as Zondervan, Thomas Nelson, Barbour, Kregel and Steeple Hill. She started writing professionally in 1977, after she completed her master's degree in history at Marshall University. Irene taught in secondary public schools for twenty-three years, but retired in 1989 to devote herself to writing.

Consistent involvement in the activities of her local church has been a source of inspiration for Irene's work. Traveling with her husband, Rod, to forty-nine of the United States, Hawaii excepted, and to thirty-two foreign countries has also inspired her writing. Irene is grateful to the many readers who have written to say that her inspiring stories and compelling portrayals of characters with strong faith have made a positive impression on their lives. You can write to her at P.O. Box 2770, Southside, WV 25187 or visit her Web site at www.irenebrand.com.

SONG OF
HER HEART

IRENE BRAND

Love Inspired.

Published by Steeple Hill Books™

STEEPLE HILL BOOKS

ISBN 0-373-87207-0

SONG OF HER HEART

Copyright © 2003 by Irene Brand

All rights reserved. Except for use in any review, the reproduction
or utilization of this work in whole or in part in any form by any
electronic, mechanical or other means, now known or hereafter
invented, including xerography, photocopying and recording, or in
any information storage or retrieval system, is forbidden without
the written permission of the editorial office, Steeple Hill Books,
300 East 42nd Street, New York, NY 10017 U.S.A.

All characters in this book have no existence outside the imagination of
the author and have no relation whatsoever to anyone bearing the same
name or names. They are not even distantly inspired by any individual
known or unknown to the author, and all incidents are pure invention.

This edition published by arrangement with Steeple Hill Books.

® and TM are trademarks of Steeple Hill Books, used under license.
Trademarks indicated with ® are registered in the United States Patent
and Trademark Office, the Canadian Trade Marks Office and in other
countries.

Visit us at www.steeplehill.com

Printed in U.S.A.

I call to remembrance my song in the night:
I commune with mine own heart:
and my spirit made diligent search.
—*Psalms* 77:6

Thanks to Myra Johnson for sharing information
about her work with SIRE,
Houston's Therapeutic Equestrian Center.

And to Charles and Elaine Rawson for sharing
expertise on how to prepare for an ox roast.

Chapter One

Norah Williamson picked up speed on the unpaved road, topped a small hill and hit the brakes with such force that the seat belt clamped her body in an unyielding grip. She panicked momentarily, finding it hard to breathe.

Blocking the roadway was the most intimidating animal she'd ever seen in her life—an enormous white-faced red bull with white patches on his chest, flanks and lower legs. Curled forward around his face were two ominous-looking horns. To Norah, the animal appeared to be gigantic as an elephant, although when she recovered from her initial shock, she realized he wasn't really that big.

Her brother's accusation flashed through Norah's mind. When Sam had learned that she'd put the family home in Springfield, Missouri, on the market and was going to take a job on a ranch in northern Nebraska, he'd said, with biting sarcasm, "You're nothing but a foolish old maid, searching for a dream that vanished twenty-five years ago."

Norah wasn't sure she'd ever forgive Sam for that remark, nor did she remind him that he was one of the reasons she'd lost her dream. But now, stranded in the middle of a sea of grassland, her way obstructed by a Hereford bull, she conceded that Sam's assessment might very well describe her situation.

After leisurely driving for two hours through Nebraska's Sand Hills, enjoying the spring flowers that dotted the fields of waving grass, pausing often to watch white-tailed deer bounding across the prairie, Norah had become a bit concerned when she realized that darkness was approaching. She'd started wondering how long it had been since she'd seen another car or even a driveway into a ranch. She'd noticed several towns of black-tailed prairie dogs, hundreds of birds on the roadside lakes and herds of white-faced cattle, but no signs of human habitation. This rangeland was overwhelming to a woman who'd lived all of her forty-two years in a city.

Her concern had lightened when she'd seen a mailbox beside the road and a sign indicating that the Flying K ranch, her destination, was three miles away. But right now she was stranded in the middle of nowhere because of this bull.

Knowing she couldn't spend the night in a stand-off with the animal, she blew the horn. He shook his head, bellowed and moved forward menacingly, shoving his huge head and shoulders over the hood of her small car. Eyeball to eyeball with the beast, she raced the engine, backed up quickly and started to pass on the right side. But instead of going forward, the car slid sideways into a deep ditch, startling a grouse from her nest in a clump of grass.

The bull ambled to the side of the road and peered down at her. Norah cowered, body trembling, expecting him to attack the car at any moment. If he did, her ten-year-old compact vehicle wouldn't provide much protection. She closed her eyes and leaned her head on the steering wheel.

"God," Norah prayed aloud, "what am I going to do? In spite of my family's displeasure with me, I'm convinced it's Your will for me to take this job. I need help."

The car was slanted at a forty-five-degree angle, and the left wheels of the vehicle were suspended several inches above the ground. She shut off the car's engine, resigned to spend the night in this position if she had to.

Opening the window a sliver, Norah detected the sound of an approaching vehicle, and saw dual headlights bounding up and down across the prairie. A red pickup ground to a halt, and a large, black-whiskered man, garbed in jeans, brown jacket, boots and a wide-brimmed hat, jumped from the truck and swatted the bull across the rear. The bull ambled to one side as the man slid down the incline toward her.

An honest-to-goodness cowboy had come to the rescue!

He bent over and peered in the window. "Ma'am, are you hurt?" he asked in a deep voice that sounded as if it came from the bottom of a well.

Relieved to know that help had come, laughing and crying at the same time, Norah gulped. "I don't think so."

When he stood, he towered over the car, and all Norah could see of her rescuer was a broad chest encased in a vivid blue shirt. The stranger quickly surveyed the situation and asked, "What happened?"

"That bull was in the middle of the road, and when I tried to drive around him, my car slid into the ditch."

"I'll have you out of there in a few minutes."

His deep, matter-of-fact voice encouraged Norah. She knew she was in safe hands, but she still didn't trust the bull.

"I'm not getting out of this car as long as that animal is here. I'm afraid of him."

The man peered in the window again, and his eyes widened in surprise. Although it was dusky, Norah could see that his eyes were almost as dark as his whiskers. "Afraid of Buster? He's gentle as a lamb."

"Ha!" she said derisively. "He shook his head and glowered at me through the windshield."

"Just Buster's way of welcoming you to the Flying K ranch. If you'd waited a few minutes, he'd have moved aside."

The stranger pulled the door open and gave Norah a strong hand to hold as she unsteadily climbed out of the car and up the steep, slippery bank.

"Then I have arrived at the Flying K ranch?"

He leaned forward and peered at Norah's face. "You headin' for the Flying K? I supposed you'd taken a wrong turn. What'd you say your name was?"

"I didn't say, but it's Norah Williamson."

The man shoved back his hat, revealing a broad forehead. A bewildered grin spread across his face, and he reached out his hand. "Well! Welcome to the Flying K ranch, Norah. I'm Mason King. Somehow I was expecting an older woman."

With those black whiskers covering three-fourths of his face, it was hard to tell how old Mason was, but the part of his face she could see was unwrinkled, his body was firm and agile and he walked with a youthful tread. She hadn't thought much about Mason's age, but it was obvious he was in his prime.

"I guess we didn't get around to exchanging ages in our e-mails," Norah said. "I'm forty-two."

"Then I'm three years ahead of you." He turned toward the ditch. "I'll soon have your car out of there. You're sure you're not hurt?"

"I don't seem to be. The car slid slowly down the hill."

"It's been raining off and on for a week, and the ground is soaked. Most times you wouldn't have had any trouble."

From his truck bed littered with a conglomeration of ranch equipment, including rope, nail kegs, wire and shovels, Mason pulled out a long chain. He attached it to her car, then fastened the chain to a hook on the back of his truck.

"Stand aside now, and I'll get your car out on the road again. There doesn't seem to be much damage."

While the pickup slowly lifted the car from the ditch, Norah kept a wary eye on Buster, now grazing contentedly in the knee-high grass beside the road. Buster glanced in her direction occasionally and let out a throaty bellow. The noise irritated her. After all, he was the reason for her misfortune, and he needn't gloat over it.

Mason circled the car, kicking at the tires and peering underneath. She couldn't tell if the car was damaged, because the whole right side was covered with mud where it had landed against the bank.

Agitated, Norah looked out into the darkness settling around them. She'd wrecked her car and was at the mercy of this stranger. Why had she made the decision to come to this remote place?

"There's a dent in one fender, but it'll run all right," Mason said. "It's too late to settle you at the Bar 8 ranch tonight, so I reckon you'll have to bunk at the Flying K. Are you okay to drive to the ranch? It's only another mile."

Still preoccupied with her awkward situation, Norah mumbled, "I'll be all right if I don't encounter another bull."

Mason answered with a pleasant laugh, and he opened the door for her. "You'll get used to cattle after you've been here a few weeks." He closed her door and got into his truck, motioning for her to follow him.

Fearing the darkness around her, Norah's hands gripped the steering wheel. The only light she could see came from the truck in front of her, and the blackness of the night in these unfamiliar surroundings intimidated her. After a short drive, Mason turned toward several buildings illuminated by security lights. He jumped from the truck and waved Norah to a parking space beside him.

''I'm not fixed for company,'' he explained as he opened the car door, ''but we can manage tonight. Wait until I get a light turned on in the house, and then I'll help you carry in what you need for overnight.''

''Do you live here alone?'' Norah asked, hoping the agitation she felt didn't register in her voice.

''Yes.''

The low, rambling house had a wide veranda running the length of the building. When Mason turned on a light, despite Norah's concern, the old, one-story weathered home seemed to welcome her.

Mason was at her side again by the time she stepped out of the car. ''I won't need anything except that small case,'' she said, indicating a piece of luggage on the floor.

He peered inside the loaded car. ''Looks like you came to stay, all right,'' he said with approval.

''I hardly knew what I'd need, so I prepared for every possibility.''

Norah entered a room that spread across the front of the house—kitchen, dining and living area were combined into one open space. It was definitely a man's home. Hunting trophies were displayed over the stone mantel that topped a cavernous fireplace.

A wide-screen television was placed where it could be seen from the kitchen table or from a large lounge chair arranged between the television and the fireplace. The walls were lined with plaques attesting to the Flying K's superiority in cattle raising.

Cereal and cracker boxes, and peanut butter and jelly jars were on the table. Stacks of newspapers and magazines covered a large library table. The room was a combination of antique and new items, including a modern refrigerator, stove, microwave and an extensive computer center.

"Have you had your supper?" Mason asked.

"I stopped in Broken Bow for a late-afternoon lunch," Norah said. "I'm not really hungry."

"Well, I am," Mason said. "I've been out on the range all day, and I didn't take time to eat. I'll rustle up something and you can eat with me. Let me show you to a bedroom."

Carrying her bag, he went down the hall ahead of her and opened a door into a small room that was sparsely furnished with a bed, dresser, two chairs and a table.

"I don't have company often," he apologized, "so the bed isn't ready for sleeping. There are sheets and pillowcases in the dresser. A neighbor comes in once a month to clean the house, and she was here last week, so the room should be all right."

"I'll be fine," Norah assured him. "If I'd realized

how far it was to the ranch, I'd have stayed in Broken Bow. I'm sorry to impose on you."

"No bother!" he assured her. "If you can manage tonight, we'll make better arrangements tomorrow. The bathroom's across the hall. Come into the kitchen when you're ready."

He went out and closed the door and Norah stood in the middle of the room, not knowing what to do. She'd be spending the night unchaperoned in the house with Mason King. Norah wasn't a prude, but Mason *was* a stranger to her—a man she'd contacted a month ago on the Internet. Norah had counted on finding a motel where she could spend the night. She hadn't realized how sparsely settled Nebraska's Sand Hills were, and she'd arrived at the Flying K ranch before she found a motel. There wasn't anything else to do but to make the best of an awkward situation.

After living all of her life surrounded by family, what had prompted her to strike out on her own to cook for a rehabilitation organization experimenting in equine therapy for children with special needs? Sam might have been right—maybe she was a foolish old maid.

She hung her jacket on a clothing rack in the corner of the room and took a set of sheets, pillowcases and a blanket from the dresser. The linens felt cold and she laid them on the bed. She'd make the bed later.

A tantalizing scent of cooking beef welcomed her return to the kitchen. "Anything I can do to help?" she offered.

"It's all ready," Mason said. "I use the microwave a lot." The two plates he placed on the wooden table held steaks and baked potatoes. He took a loaf of bread, a carton of butter and a deli container of coleslaw from the refrigerator.

"Think this is enough to hold you until morning?"

"More than enough."

Mason pulled out a chair for Norah, sat opposite her and bowed his head. "God, thank You for giving Norah a safe journey. We ask Your guidance for this project we're undertaking. Thanks for the food and bless it to our body's use. Amen."

Mason's prayer, indicating a deep spiritual devotion, set Norah's mind at ease about the propriety of spending the night in his home. She settled back to enjoy her meal.

"I don't know why you advertised for a cook," she said. "This food is delicious."

"I can't run a cattle ranch *and* cook for a bunch of kids. Besides, I'm a meat-and-potatoes guy. Anything else is beyond me. My friends Doug and Sheila Johnson live on my other ranch, and they invite me for a good meal about every week. I eat out whenever I go to town, but the rest of the time I just get by."

After they'd eaten, refusing Norah's offer of help, Mason efficiently cleared the table and put their dishes and utensils in the dishwasher.

"The days are still cool, so I like a fire in the evenings." He turned the lounge chair to face the fireplace, placed another comfortable chair beside it for Norah and held a match to the stacked wood.

"Let's sit and relax while we get acquainted."

"That's a good idea. I'm not an impulsive person, so I even surprised myself when I accepted this job without learning more about what I was getting into."

Nodding, Mason answered, "I'm sometimes impulsive, too. For instance, I bought a dude ranch, the Bar 8, which adjoins my property, about four years ago. I operated it as a dude ranch for two summers, which was nothing but an aggravation to me. I couldn't find good help, and I was spending time entertaining city people when I should have been taking care of my cattle."

One of the logs crumbled and sparks wafted up the chimney. A puff of smoke fanned out into the room, and Mason rearranged the firewood with a poker.

"I'd already listed the property for sale," Mason

continued, "when Horses and Healing, a Christian group of therapists in Omaha, contacted me, asking to use the ranch for a pilot project in equine therapy for children with special needs. They offered a good rent for the summer months, and when I learned my only obligation was to provide horses and a cook for the riders and volunteers, I temporarily took the property off the market. When you answered my ad and said that you'd taken care of your handicapped brother, I figured you'd relate to the children and not find it difficult to work with them."

"Because of my experience with Billy, I'm very interested in any program designed to make life better for children with special needs. I was at loose ends after my father and brother both died this past winter. When I saw your ad, I felt it was the place for me. I needed a job, and since I'd managed our home after my mother died twenty-five years ago, I felt I was qualified."

"I'm sure you are, and it'll be a pleasure to have you here," Mason said. "If we can make a difference in the lives of a few children, it'll be worth the work. And we'll also be serving Jesus, for He said, 'Whatever you've done for one of these little ones, you've done to me.'"

"I believe that, too. I've been thinking of the summer's work as a ministry rather than a job."

If it was too late to realize her goal of serving as

Chapter Two

Although he'd had a long, hard day, Mason mused before the fire for more than an hour after Norah went to bed. The pleasant murmur of her velvet voice revolved over and over in his mind, a comforting sound that had wiggled its way into the loneliness of his heart. This was the first time a woman had spent the night in his home since his wife had died years ago, a few hours after she'd delivered their stillborn child.

Mason had longed for children, and the possibility of remarriage had often crossed his mind. He'd stopped mourning his young wife long ago, and he would have married if only he'd found a woman to spark his interest. For a few years, he'd considered getting married just so he could have a family, and he'd dated, but he couldn't bring himself to propose to a woman he didn't love.

Mason had believed it was important for him to marry because he was an only child and had no children. He often worried about what would happen to the Flying K after his death. He and his father had spent their lives building up this property, and he didn't want the ranch to pass to someone he didn't know.

But when he reached forty, Mason had decided that he'd passed the age when he could satisfactorily rear a child, and he'd put the idea of marriage on the back burner. But now Norah had come!

Was her arrival providential? He'd received six answers to his Internet ad, but none of the messages had seemed right until Norah had written. He took her message from his desk and read it again.

> Mr. King,
> Having cared for my father and siblings, including a disabled brother, for several years, I believe I qualify for the job you mentioned in your ad. I've never been employed outside the home, so I can't supply work references. The pastor of my church can furnish a character recommendation.

She'd given the pastor's name and e-mail address, but Mason hadn't contacted the man. He and Norah had corresponded several times by e-mail, and he'd anticipated her arrival with pleasure. Mason had envisioned Norah as a woman in her sixties, who would provide a grandmotherly model for the children in the therapeutic program.

Norah didn't impress him as the grandmotherly type. He could hardly believe she was forty-two years old. Her straight, silvery-gray hair—no doubt prematurely gray—was neatly arranged over her forehead in a wispy mist, then flowed neatly in soft layers to the base of her neck. Her bright, clear-blue eyes were highlighted by long, black lashes that created a startling contrast as they caressed her well-modeled ivory face. She was of medium height with a winsome body.

Being a large man, Mason had never been attracted to petite, delicate women who looked like a strong prairie wind would blow them away. Norah Williamson filled the physical qualities he admired in a woman—although not obese, she carried enough flesh that a man could have an armful when he hugged her.

While they'd sat at the table visiting, and later relaxing by the fire, Mason realized that, for the first time, this house seemed like a home. His mother had died when Mason was a child, and he didn't even remember her. During the year he'd been married, he and his wife had lived in a small house a few miles away. After her death, he'd moved in with his father. Mason had been lonely since his father's death, but he hadn't understood how lonely until Norah had entered his home. Yearnings that Mason thought he'd stifled forever suddenly seemed important again, and he stayed in his easy chair long after the embers of the fire had faded away.

The room was totally dark when Norah awakened, and she was terrified. Realization came quickly that she wasn't in her bed at home, but on an isolated ranch in northern Nebraska. The awareness did nothing to calm her nerves. She hastily turned on the light that was hooked over the wooden headboard of the bed, and her racing heartbeat eased when the light chased the darkness away.

She lifted her watch from the bedside table. Four o'clock! After spending a restless night, Norah longed for daylight and the start of a new day. She'd still been awake when Mason had entered his bedroom across the hallway, and although she'd dozed several times, thoughts of Mason had been present in her mind all night.

Occupied as she'd been with caring for her family, Norah hadn't made many male friends, so she was unprepared for her physical reaction to Mason's rugged personality. His wide shoulders were slightly stooped, but his rangy body towered several inches over six feet. Obviously a powerful man, Mason was a product of the rangeland where he and his ancestors had battled the elements to make a home. His black whiskers and hair were tinged with gray, and his generous mouth and dark brown eyes were touched with humor. But in spite of his vigorous masculinity, she detected a hint of wistfulness in Mason's gentle expression, as if he was searching for something that evaded him. He obviously was a successful rancher, but was he happy?

Disgusted that she'd allowed thoughts of Mason to keep her awake, Norah flopped over on her side and hoped for sleep, but concern about the uncertainty of her future wouldn't let her rest.

She was committed to working for Mason during the summer, but what then? Knowing that she didn't have enough education to become a missionary kept Norah wide-awake. She'd hoped to use the money from the sale of the family home to prepare for her lifelong dream of becoming a missionary. But was she too old to work on the overseas mission field? It would take several years to receive the education she needed for mission appointment, and by that time she'd be almost fifty years old. What could a woman in midlife do to make her life count?

Hearing a soft knock on the door, Norah roused from her catnap.

"Yes," she answered sleepily.

"I'm going to the barn," Mason said. "I'll be back in an hour, and we can have breakfast. But if you're tired, go back to sleep."

"No, I'm ready to get up."

The room was cold, and after she heard Mason's deliberate tread outside the window, Norah put on her robe and hustled into the bathroom across the hall. After a shower, she put on the extra change of clothes she'd packed in the small bag. A pair of jeans and a plaid, long-sleeved shirt seemed suitable attire for a ranch cook, she thought humorously as she walked toward the kitchen.

From the many boxes of dry cereal on the table, she concluded Mason didn't often have a hot breakfast. The refrigerator contained what she needed to prepare an omelette and mix a batch of bread. She put the biscuits in the oven, thinking she could warm them in the microwave if they baked before Mason finished his work. She found honey and oleo in the fridge and put them on the table, made a pot of coffee and prepared a pan for the omelette. Ready to finish breakfast when Mason came, Norah sat on a wide window seat to watch for him.

Low rolling hills surrounded the Flying K ranch that was located in the Niobrara River Valley. A large red barn with a tall silo attached and several smaller buildings were near the house. A wide shelter belt of evergreens was positioned to protect the ranch headquarters from northwest winter winds. Sunlight was just beginning to illuminate the meadowy fields where a herd of cattle grazed, and Norah wondered if Buster was among them. In the light of day, her fear of the bull seemed a little foolish, but the sudden sight of him in the middle of the road had overwhelmed her.

When Mason emerged from the barn, he was accompanied by two black Labrador dogs that frolicked at his heels all the way to the house. When Norah opened the door and said, "Good morning," the dogs froze in place. Mason stooped to lay calming hands on their heads.

"It's okay," he assured the animals. Smiling at Norah, he continued. "Around here, the dogs get their breakfast before I do." He dipped some dry dog food from a container and filled a couple of bowls. He turned on a faucet and replenished the dogs' water pans. Patting their heads again, he stepped inside and came to a standstill, almost as quickly as the dogs had done.

"You've made breakfast!"

"Why not? You need a sample of my cooking to see if I'm suited for the job. If not, you can hire someone else before the kids come to the ranch."

Smiling, he said, "If the food tastes as good as it smells, I won't want to hire anyone else."

"Everything's finished except the omelette. I'll have it on the table by the time you've washed up."

"Even biscuits!" Mason marveled as he returned from the bathroom and pulled up to the table. "I make biscuits once in a while, but they don't look like these."

Since he usually ate alone, Mason didn't talk much while he ate three-fourths of the omelette, several biscuits and downed two cups of coffee. By the time only one biscuit was left on the plate, Norah didn't need any more evidence that her cooking passed muster.

When Mason leaned back from the table, with a satisfied smile on his face, Norah filled his coffee cup for the third time.

"I've never eaten a better meal in my life," Mason said. "Thanks, Norah. If the therapy program doesn't improve the kids' health, eating your meals is bound to be good for them. Thanks for coming to help."

A song rose in Norah's heart at his praise. In spite of her efforts to please her family, she'd seldom had any thanks for what she'd done for them. Her father had paid her for taking care of the household, but it always rankled that her family had taken her work for granted.

Unbidden, an old adage popped into Norah's mind. *The way to a man's heart is through his stom-*

ach. But why would she want to find her way into Mason's heart? The goal she'd set for her life when she was a teenager couldn't be realized on a Sand Hills ranch. And although she'd known Mason only a few hours, she couldn't envision him in any other place except this setting.

Mason interrupted her thoughts when he said, "I'll take you to the Bar 8 ranch today so you can see where you'll be spending the summer. The program doesn't start for two weeks. You may not want to stay there all that time."

"How far away is the Bar 8 ranch?"

"About ten miles."

"Anyone live closer than that?"

"One of my employees and his wife live on the property as caretakers, three-quarters of a mile from the main house. I graze cattle and horses on the ranch, and we occasionally have rustlers, so I can't leave the property unprotected."

Norah had always lived in a city and didn't look forward to staying at the isolated Bar 8. But where else could she stay? There weren't any motels close by, and she certainly couldn't spend two weeks at the Flying K. This was one hurdle she hadn't considered in her hasty decision to accept the job.

"I'll look around the Bar 8 before I decide where to stay. I'll need to check out the kitchen facilities and start planning meals. The only time I've cooked for a large group has been on holidays. I'll need to plan well in advance, so I'll know what groceries to buy.''

"Then you should drive your car to the Bar 8, in case you do want to move in today, and I'll follow in the truck. Otherwise, we could have gone on horseback. There's a nice trail between the two ranches, and I'd rather ride a horse than drive, but trucks are a lot faster.''

Norah slanted her eyes toward him. She'd never ridden a horse, but she figured that was something she'd learn to do before the summer was over. Would she regret her hasty decision to take this job?

Pulling his chair up to the table again, Mason reached for the last biscuit. "I might as well eat this. It looks lonesome on that plate all by itself.''

The two-story frame white house at the Bar 8 ranch gleamed in the morning sun. As they stood in the yard, Mason explained, "This place was a horse ranch for years, and the house was built sometime before World War I when ranching was profitable. But after the original owners died, a man from Colorado bought the property and developed it into a vacation ranch for city people.''

Norah followed Mason's pointing hand as he said, "He turned the barn loft into dormitories and kept the ground floor as a meeting room and dance hall.''

"Will these children be able to use second-floor facilities?"

"No, but that motel-like building beside the barn has several rooms. The staff will use the barn loft for offices, the first floor as an inside riding arena, and the one-story building will be used to lodge the children and volunteers. Those other buildings are the stables and equipment sheds."

He turned his attention to the house. "Let's go inside so you can see where you'll be working."

A newly installed ramp made the house handicapped accessible. When the house was renovated for use as a dude ranch, partitions had been taken out of the original structure and the first floor contained a kitchen, a large dining area and rest rooms to the left of the dining room.

"The kitchen equipment is modern," Norah commented as she looked around the large room.

"Yes, it's in good shape. The upstairs rooms haven't changed much since the house was built."

"Hey, Mason," a voice called from outside.

"That's Doug. I'll see what he wants."

Mason opened the door. A young blond man, dressed in jeans and a flannel shirt, stood on the porch. "Doug, meet Norah Williamson. She's the one I hired to take care of the cooking." He turned to Norah and explained, "Doug Johnson and his wife, Sheila, are the caretakers here. Sheila will be helping you in the kitchen.''

"Glad to meet you, Norah," Doug said, taking off his wide-brimmed hat. "Sheila's been looking forward to your arrival." Looking at Mason, he said, "Before you leave, I'd like for you to come to the stable. I brought in an injured calf—thought you'd better take a look at it."

"I can check the rest of the house by myself, if you want to go now," Norah said to Mason.

"All right. I'll stop back soon and see what you've decided."

The upstairs was divided into four bedrooms and two bathrooms. All the rooms were furnished comfortably with choices of queen or twin beds, and plenty of chairs and chests. Norah chose a room with a queen-size bed on the back side of the house for her personal quarters. She was downstairs giving the kitchen a closer inspection when Mason returned.

"This kitchen is supplied with anything a cook would need, but I want to wash all the utensils and dishes before the guests arrive. I'll have plenty to keep me occupied for the next two weeks. We might as well move in my things, and then you can go back to your work."

"You don't have to clean the house. Sheila does it occasionally, but H & H has arranged for volunteers to do the cleaning. You're not required to do anything except cook.''

"Still, I'll have enough to keep me busy until the children arrive.''

"But I've gotten the feeling that you're a little uneasy about living in the country. Will you be afraid to stay alone?''

"Probably, but I'll get used to it. Don't worry about me.''

Mason's eyes still reflected his concern after the car was unpacked. "I'll leave my cell phone with you until phone service can be started here.'' He took a sale bill from his pocket and wrote Doug's phone number as well as his own on it and handed the paper to Norah. "If you have any trouble at all, call me. Will you promise to do that?''

"All right, Mason, I promise.''

She stood on the porch and waved to him as he drove away. After spending her life caring for others, it was nice to have someone concerned about her. In less than twenty-four hours, Mason had brought a song to her heart—a song of thanksgiving to God for bringing this man into her life.

She watched until Mason reached the county road, where he made a quick U-turn and came back to the house. She went down the steps to meet him.

"Is something wrong?''

He pushed his hat far back on his forehead.

"We're not thinking too well. There's no food here, unless you have groceries packed in your suitcases."

"I have some fruit and crackers in the car." Norah laughed and patted her stomach. "But it won't hurt me to fast for a few hours. If you'll give me directions to a grocery store, I'll go shopping tomorrow and lay in a supply of food to last me until our guests arrive."

Mason scratched his head, an unconscious mannerism he displayed when he was thinking. "I've got some work to finish today, but tomorrow I can take you into Valentine and show you where to shop."

"I don't want to inconvenience you. I'll find my way if you point me in the right direction." She added, in a joking manner, "That is, if I don't encounter Buster again."

"I told you that Buster is a lamb. Actually, I'm trying to think of a way to keep you at my house for a few days. After that breakfast you prepared, I want to see what you can do with a full meal."

"Then I'll settle in here today, come to your ranch, prepare supper, spend the night and tomorrow we'll go shopping. How's that?"

A wide smile spread over his face, and his whiskers seemed to bristle with pleasure.

"That's music to my ears. If I'm not at home

when you arrive, go on in. The door's never locked. The freezer is full of meat."

Mason's gaze roved over the secluded valley that surrounded the Bar 8, and he reflected, "For the past four years I've often considered this ranch a pain in the neck." He looked pointedly at her, and his dark eyes were gentle and contemplative as he added, "Today it looks better to me than it ever has."

His words brought a glow of warmth to her face, and her heart sang with delight as he stepped into the pickup and drove away.

Chapter Three

Norah had just started checking out the kitchen appliances when a knock sounded on the door. A petite brunette entered at Norah's invitation.

"Hi," the newcomer said. "I'm Sheila Johnson, Doug's wife. I'll be your closest neighbor. Is there anything I can help you do today?"

"I hardly know what to do myself," Norah admitted. "Mason seems vague about the rehab program. Have you talked with any of the staff members about their planned schedule?"

"Yes, a little." Sheila shivered. "It's cold in here. We need more heat to take out the dampness. Come in the dining room, and I'll turn up the thermostat. I run the sweeper and dust once a month, but I haven't been here for three weeks."

Heat soon penetrated the house as Sheila and Norah sat on the sofa located at one end of the large dining room.

"The equine therapeutic program is called Horses and Healing," Sheila explained, "better known by H & H. Their activities start the first of June and will end by September. That's about all I've been told. I have the telephone number of the Omaha office if you want to talk with the director."

"I'll do that. I've never handled a job like this," Norah admitted, "and I'm a little anxious about it. I want to be well prepared before the first group arrives."

Sheila stood. "Let me know when I can help you. Will you come to our house for supper this evening?"

"Thanks, but I'm going back to Mason's tonight, and he'll take me into town tomorrow. I need to buy groceries for myself until the therapy sessions start." A smile touched Norah's shapely mouth. "He invited me to supper, but I have to prepare it. He mentioned meat, but I wonder what else he has to cook."

Sheila laughed. "Precious little! He keeps meat, potatoes and apples, but not much else. He'd starve to death if he had to depend on his own cooking. He goes to town several times a week, and he always stops in at a restaurant."

"He mentioned that you invite him to dinner often."

Sheila's eyes gleamed fondly. "Yes, we do. Doug's father and Mason have been friends for years. He's almost like one of the family."

"I'm sure he appreciates it."

"By the way, I keep a well-stocked pantry and freezer, because sometimes in the winter we're snowbound and I can't go to the store for a week or more. Come to our house for lunch, and you can choose some food from the freezer to supplement what you'll find at the Flying K."

"Thanks, I'll do that. It's not easy to step into a strange kitchen and prepare a meal, although I managed breakfast this morning."

After Sheila left, Norah took an inventory of the kitchen equipment and serving dishes, but she couldn't keep her mind on the work she'd be doing throughout the summer months. Instead, she kept anticipating another evening in Mason's company.

Soon after she returned from lunching with Doug and Sheila, she packed her overnight bag and headed toward the Flying K headquarters. Sheila had contributed some fresh vegetables and other staples to supplement the supplies she'd find in Mason's kitchen.

Barking loudly, the black Labs surrounded her car

when she reached the Flying K. Their tails were wagging, and considering that a good sign, Norah got out of her car, let them sniff her hands, then scratched their backs before she went inside.

She didn't know when to expect Mason, but she figured he'd work until almost dark. She took a thick steak from the freezer, and while it thawed in the microwave, she checked out the rest of the supplies she'd need.

Three hours later, when she saw Mason, on horseback, hazing a small herd of calves toward the corral, she had the meal prepared. Swiss steak, curried rice, green beans, vegetable salad, hot rolls and custard pie should be the kind of meal he'd like. As hard as he worked, Mason would soon throw off the calories from that kind of meal, but Norah knew she'd have to eat small portions.

When had she suddenly become concerned about the extra ten or fifteen pounds she carried? Oh, just in the past twenty-four hours! Admiration of Mason's muscular body had prompted her to take a closer look at herself, making her wish she still weighed the same as she had twenty years ago.

All day long, Mason had looked forward to another evening with Norah. While he rounded up calves for branding, he kept remembering how well she'd fit into his environment. It hadn't seemed awkward to have a strange woman sitting at the table. He couldn't recall when he'd ever met a woman who put him more at ease. Living alone as he did, he'd talk for hours when he met one of his male acquaintances, but he never had much to say to women.

He'd used the excuse of a meal to persuade her to spend another night at the Flying K, although it wasn't the food, but Norah's company that he wanted.

After he'd thought about it, Mason figured Norah had hesitated to accept his invitation because she wasn't comfortable staying in the house with him. He supposed he should have thought of that. *He* knew she was safe with him, but she had no way of knowing what kind of man he was. He'd wondered all day if she would really come, but his heart beat a little faster, and he jiggled the reins for added speed, when he topped a small rise and saw her white car parked in front of his home.

Norah was standing on the porch, and she waved as he drove the calves into the corral. He hustled to finish his evening chores, so eager to see Norah that he didn't even think about food until he stepped up on the porch. It was such a change to smell food cooking when he approached the house that he halted abruptly. What had he missed all of these years by not having a wife waiting for him at the end of his day's work?

Norah smiled easily, and Mason's smile, gleaming from his bewhiskered face, matched hers in contentment when she appeared at the door, dressed in a red blouse and tan pants.

"Good evening, Mason. You work late."

Mason had never experienced such a pleasurable homecoming. If she'd been his wife, he could have taken her in his arms and kissed her, but he only said, "There's always a lot of work on a ranch in the spring. I usually have a man or two working with me, but no one could help today. Smells like you've got a fine supper waiting. I haven't eaten since morning, so I hope you fixed plenty."

"I don't think you'll go away from the table hungry."

And he didn't. When the meal was finished, dishes put away, they sat down to relax. He'd forgotten how much pleasure a wife could bring to a home. He'd only lived one year with his wife, and that had been a long time ago. Besides, she'd been ill most of that time carrying their child, and they hadn't had much opportunity to enjoy each other's company.

Just two days of Norah's presence, and he'd started thinking of marriage again. He'd told himself, over and over, during the past twenty-four hours that his thoughts were ridiculous. He knew they were, but he could see no reason not to enjoy Norah's company to the fullest when he could.

Wanting to learn all he could about her, Mason asked, "What about your family, Norah? Your childhood?"

Norah's dark eyebrows curved mischievously. "You've already hired me. It's a little late for a background check."

He countered her lighthearted mood by saying, "After that feast tonight, regardless of your credentials, you won't get fired. I'll kidnap you if I have to, just to have you cook for me."

"But when Horses and Healing starts operating, I'll be cooking for them," she responded. An eyebrow tilted provocatively, and her lips trembled slightly in amusement.

"Surely you won't turn me away if I come around for an occasional handout."

"We'll see," she said, her azure eyes sparkling with silent laughter. "But about my childhood," she continued, seriously, "it's been so long ago that I can hardly remember. Actually, I had a fine childhood but my mother was killed in an automobile accident when I was almost eighteen. I grew up mighty fast after that."

"My mother died when I was two. I can't even remember her."

"Oh, I'm sorry!"

"My dad made up for it, though. He didn't marry again and devoted his time to me. But go ahead with your story."

"There were five of us. I was ten years older than the other children, so Dad asked me to take over managing the house after Mother's death. I didn't hesitate to do that, although it was a great disappointment when I couldn't go to college as I'd planned."

"What was wrong with your disabled brother?"

"Billy had cerebral palsy, and I cared for him as my mother would have done." Her lips quivered as she added, "He died six months ago, a month before my father. My other brother and two sisters were away from home by that time. The work I'd spent over half of my life doing was suddenly taken away, and I was at loose ends. I admit that I'd chafed at my lifestyle—often thinking I was in bondage. But when I had my freedom, I didn't know what to do with it."

Norah paused, and her thoughts filtered back to the time when her whole life seemed to collapse around her. "While I was casting around for some direction, I came across your e-mail advertisement. Coming to do this work seemed like an opportunity to get away from familiar surroundings for a few months and find a new perspective on what I can do with the rest of my life.''

''What do you want to do?''

''Become a missionary,'' she said simply. ''That's all I've ever wanted to do. I was fifteen when I experienced God's call to go overseas as a missionary. By the time I graduated from high school, I'd been accepted at a Christian college. My training would have started a month after my mother was killed.''

''Are you going on with that training now?'' Mason asked, with some disappointment. His dreams of a future with Norah had been nipped in the bud before they'd hardly materialized in his own mind.

''I don't know. I'm kind of apprehensive about starting college at my age. I'd be almost fifty before I could get the necessary education and training. And I'm not sure I could receive an appointment at that age.''

''It seems a bit selfish of your father to ask you to give up the career you'd planned.''

''I've never blamed him. He couldn't care for Billy by himself, and none of us wanted to put Billy in an institution, so I was happy to do it. But I fully expected, when my siblings became older, that they would assume some of the responsibilities and free me to go to college, but none of them even considered it.''

"Did you ask them?"

"Yes, of course, and they'd give me half promises, then pursue their own lives as if they had no obligation to their family. I'd been a mother to them, and I'm ashamed to admit that I find it hard to forgive them for being so insensitive to my needs."

"It does seem as if they could have helped."

Norah leaned back and closed her eyes. "You would think so, but they didn't. In fact, they compounded my problem by using me as a baby-sitter. They knew I'd always be at home, so they brought their children to me for an afternoon, a day, sometimes as long as a week while they went on vacation. It didn't seem to occur to them that I might like a break. My father took over so I could attend church services, but I didn't even do that after Billy's health worsened."

"Sounds like your siblings are selfish."

She opened her eyes and nodded. "Yes, they are. And they're so mad at me now that they won't speak to me. My father willed the family home to me, and they didn't mind at all because they thought the situation would continue as always. But I put the house up for sale several weeks ago. I might use the money from selling the house to go to college, but that depends on whether I'm too old to still realize my dream."

Mason slanted a speculative glance in her direction. "So that's why they're mad at you!"

"Yes. Their free baby-sitter is gone." She paused, thinking of the quarrel she'd had with her family. "The things they said to me hurt deeply—words that I find hard to forgive."

"Sounds to me like you've done enough for them."

"I suppose so, but I keep remembering that Jesus taught His followers to be servants. He said once, 'Whatever you did for one of the least of these brothers of mine, you did for me.' And the Apostle Paul made a strong point when he said, 'Serve one another in love.' So I'm probably a disobedient Christian by resenting the years I spent serving my family."

"I assume your siblings are Christians, too. Looks like serving ought to work both ways," Mason argued in her defense.

"I've tried to justify my attitude, using the same line of reasoning, but my conscience makes me wonder if the mission field God had in mind for me was serving in my own home. I did my duty by taking care of Dad and my brother, but maybe I was doing it for the wrong reasons."

"I don't believe that for a minute," Mason said. "I've only known you for a short time, but I'm convinced you're a loving, compassionate woman."

"Thanks, Mason. I'd like to believe that, but when I take an introspective look at myself, I don't like what I see. I pray that this summer's work will give me a new perspective on what God wants me to do. With all my heart, I want to accept His will for my life."

Mason watched the play of emotions on Norah's face, and as she sat with eyes downcast, he wanted to put a comforting hand on her shoulder. But now wasn't the time. Nor would it be appropriate to tell Norah that the longer he was around her, the more he liked what he saw.

Chapter Four

The two dogs jumped on Mason as he and Norah exited the door the next morning. He wrestled playfully with them for a few minutes.

"Okay, you guys are in charge," he said. "We'll be gone most of the day. I'm taking Norah on a tour of the county."

He opened the truck door for Norah. There wasn't a running board, which meant she had to manage a step of almost two feet to get into the vehicle. Mason pushed back his hat and scratched his head, a habitual gesture of his.

"Well, now!" he said. "I swing into the truck seat like I mount a horse. That *is* a big step for a lady."

Without a word, he put his arms around Norah's

waist and effortlessly placed her on the seat. She sensed the warmth of his large hands through her shirt.

"If I'm going to ride in your truck, you'll have to bring a ladder along for me," she said, when he swung into the driver's seat and started the engine.

Grinning provocatively, he said lazily, "Oh, I don't know. I kinda liked the way we did it this morning."

Flustered, Norah looked out the window and waved a hand at the dogs, who were standing downhearted, tails between their legs, watching them leave.

"The dogs like to ride in the truck, but not when I leave the ranch."

"What're their names?"

"Pete and Repeat."

"What!"

"I got them when they were pups. They're from the same litter and almost identical, so I thought those were good names. They're good hunters. We have lots of water fowl in this area."

Mason threaded his fingers through his bushy beard. "I don'tknow if I can stand these whiskers for six more weeks. They're about to drive me crazy."

"Then you don't usually wear whiskers?"

"Never have before! Ranchers in this end of the

county gather on the Fourth of July for horse racing, fireworks, music, ox roast—that sort of thing. We try to revive the Old West for a day. We give prizes for the most authentic costumes, and for riding contests. But last year, somebody came up with the crazy idea of having a beard-growing contest to see who could grow the most outstanding beard from New Year's Day to the Fourth of July. I didn't mind it so much when the weather was cold, but whiskers are too hot for summer. I'm tempted to shave now and be done with it.''

"Oh, I wouldn't do that," Norah said as the truck whizzed past the spot where she'd had the encounter with Buster.

"Do you like my whiskers?" he asked, a quizzical expression in his eyes.

A flash of humor spread across her face. "Not particularly, but you've put up with them this long, you shouldn't give up now. They might not be so bad if you'd trim them.''

"I might as well shave completely as trim the beard. We're judged on who has the longest and thickest whiskers.''

"Then, by all means, don't trim them. I believe in finishing what you start. Since you've had the whiskers for almost five months, you might as well keep them on until after the contest.''

They met a few other pickups as they traveled

northward toward Valentine, and Norah noticed that all the male drivers had beards.

"Where do you have the celebration?"

"Each rancher takes turns hosting the event, and it'll be at the Flying K this summer. A committee plans the day's activities, so all I have to do is supply the place and the meat. I'll provide a steer."

"Sounds like fun."

"You're invited to come. Ranchers' clothes haven't changed much in the last hundred years, but the women wear vintage outfits. I think you can rent costumes in Valentine."

"I'd like to be there, but it will depend on my duties for Horses and Healing."

"I don't believe they're in session during the holiday week," he said. "I'd like for you to be my hostess for the occasion."

"What does a hostess have to do?"

"Welcome people to the party by serving coffee or soft drinks when they arrive. Mostly, just see that everyone has a good time. Since I live alone, my guests have always fended for themselves when they came to the Flying K."

"I'll consider it. How many attend?"

"Fifty to seventy-five. We aren't heavily populated in this part of the state."

Mason had attended all of the celebrations. The

miles passed quickly as he entertained Norah with amusing anecdotes of past years.

When they entered the outskirts of Valentine, Mason said, "The town is known as Nebraska's Heart City. People from all over the world send valentines to be stamped and mailed from here. But it's a thriving town, too, serving the ranchers in this vicinity."

They went first to a garage where Norah made arrangements for repair to be made on her car the next week. Then Mason drove around the business section, pointing out the post office, several grocery stores and restaurants. They stopped at a bank so Norah could open an account, which would be more convenient than to draw on her bank in Missouri during the summer. When they left the bank, Mason checked his watch.

"It's eleven o'clock," he said. "Since the weather is nice today, how about having a picnic?"

"Sounds great to me."

"Let's buy food and go to the picnic area at the Fort Niobrara National Wildlife Refuge east of town."

He drove to a grocery store that had a deli, and when they went inside, Mason said, "You order—I'll pay. I like any food, so buy what you want."

Norah ordered a large and a small sub sandwich with cheese and turkey, two containers of vegetable salad and slices of chocolate cake. She chose frosted fruit drinks, as well as a cup of coffee for Mason.

"We'll stop back here before we leave town so you can buy the groceries you need."

The thought of her move to the Bar 8 ranch depressed him. The more he was around Norah, the more she fascinated him. He wanted her to stay at the Flying K until the children arrived, but he knew he shouldn't suggest it.

He could think of numerous reasons why he shouldn't become emotionally involved with Norah, so he was only laying up heartache for himself by becoming fond of her. A little voice inside kept repeating, *Even if it's only for a short time, you might as well enjoy her.* Still, always in the back of his mind was the tickling certainty of how lonely he'd be when she left Nebraska at the end of the summer.

Mason related the background of the area as they drove the short distance to the refuge, and Norah learned that great herds of buffalo had roamed the grasslands before white settlers came to the region. The Range Indians had depended on the buffalo for their livelihood, following the great herds as they migrated from north to south for summer and winter grazing. As the United States frontier expanded westward, Fort Niobrara had been built in 1879 to discourage conflict between the natives and the settlers.

"During the twenty-some years of the fort's existence, the soldiers weren't involved in any fighting," Mason said. "And a few years after the fort was dismantled in 1912, the area became a wildlife refuge."

As Mason continued to discuss the history of the land, Norah considered what a difference a few days in Mason's company had made. Even in her thoughts, she didn't like to keep harping on how her family had imposed upon her, but for over twenty years she'd been almost like a prisoner of her family. When she did leave the house, she was always in a hurry to get home, knowing she was needed. She'd had a few boyfriends in her teen years, and they'd gone to movies and eaten in the local restaurants, but she hadn't dated at all after her mother died. And she'd hardly set foot out of Springfield during all those years.

Travel commentaries hadn't prepared her for the beauty of America. She looked in awe at the rolling Sand Hills and the breaks along the Niobrara River. Wild turkeys scratched in the grasslands along the river, where aspen and burr oak trees grew, side by side with Ponderosa pines. Near the Visitor's Center, prairie dogs lived in an underground town, and several peered out of holes and barked. Mason lowered the windows so they could listen to meadowlarks, perched on fence posts, serenading them as they drove by.

"Why are there so few trees?" Norah asked.

"The soil is sandy, there's not much rainfall and strong winds through the centuries have discouraged tree growth."

A large herd of buffalo, almost every cow with a brownish-colored calf by her side, grazed contentedly in the high grass along the river. As they traveled slowly along the wildlife drive, Norah made constant use of Mason's binoculars, which he always kept in the glove compartment, sighting elk, and Texas longhorn cattle, also with calves by their sides.

"The refuge is devoted primarily to the management of buffalo, elk and Texas longhorns," Mason explained. "Although millions of buffalo once roamed the grasslands, the animals had dwindled to less than a thousand in the United States until these programs started. The wildlife are kept at manageable numbers—four hundred buffalo, sixty elk and about three hundred longhorns—here in this refuge. Other areas in the country have similar programs."

"It's great to see our nation's tax dollars put to such a good use. A lot of the nation's history would have disappeared without programs like this."

"Several hiking trails lead into the wilder areas of the refuge, but we won't have time to hike today," Mason said as he parked the truck and they got out. "Let's eat, buy your groceries and head home."

They placed the deli containers on a picnic table, but with the wind blowing at hurricane force, it was a constant battle to prevent the sandwich wrappers from blowing away.

With a wry grimace, Mason said, "Not too good a day for a picnic, but the wind always blows up here."

Holding a juice carton in her left hand, and a sub in the other, Norah couldn't do anything about her hair that was standing straight up. A particularly strong gust lifted Mason's hat from his head and pitched it several yards away. He hurriedly retrieved the hat and threw it into the truck, allowing his long hair to blow around his face.

A lot of women would be having a fit about having to eat under such conditions, Mason thought, but Norah downed her food without complaint. He looked her over approvingly, caressing her with his dark eyes.

Norah intercepted his gaze, and her face flushed. Why couldn't she get over acting like a lovesick youth when she was with this man? It was disturbing to blush every time he favored her with a glance.

Noting her heightened color, Mason said, "I shouldn't have been staring. It's so unusual for me to be out having a good time in the middle of a workday, that I keep wondering if it's really happening or if I'm dreaming."

"It's sort of like a dream for me, too. We have

excellent scenery in Missouri, but I haven't seen much of it. I'm a vicarious traveler. I've read a lot of books on our national parks and I watch travelogues on TV, but it seems different when you're actually on the site. This has been a rare treat for me today. So, thanks, Mason.''

"Didn't you get away from home at all?"

"Not for overnight. Most of my expeditions were concerned with shopping, doctors' appointments and the like. The years passed before I knew it.''

"Ranchers can't take extended vacations, so I haven't done much traveling, either. But I've hunted in Wyoming and Colorado, and I know the Dakotas and Nebraska pretty well.''

"Don't think I'm complaining about my years at home. I was willing to do it. But that's all I've done, so I don't have much of interest to talk about.''

"Talk about anything that pops into your head," Mason said. "I enjoy the sound of your voice.''

Not wanting a repeat performance of being lifted bodily into the truck, Norah had learned to stand on tiptoe, hold the door handle and spring into the truck cab, while Mason stood by if she needed help. She was sure she didn't look very graceful, but at least she had managed the two times she'd boarded the truck in Valentine. But this time, she fell backward against Mason. He wrapped his arms around her midriff, and for a moment, she relaxed against him, enjoying the feel of his arms around her. Her breath was uneven, but she said, shakily, "Perhaps you'd better give me a boost."

He loosened his grip lightly and lifted her into the cab. Refusing to meet his gaze, Norah took a comb from her purse and arranged her hair in its usual style. Mason shook his head to settle his hair in place before he put on his hat.

"My hair is as hard to control as my beard," he said. "I've been letting it grow along with my whiskers. I think I'll dress as a mountain man for this year's celebration, if I can find a buckskin outfit to fit me."

When he pulled into the parking lot in front of a grocery store, he said, "This is where Sheila does all of her buying, so I guess it's a good place. I keep a cooler in the back of the truck during the summer months, so you can take perishables back with you. While you shop, I'll buy a sack of ice and dump it in the cooler."

"I won't buy much," Norah said as she went into the store. "Just enough to tide me over until I have the job outline for the summer."

Mason stopped at the Flying K long enough for Norah to pick up her car, and then he continued to the Bar 8 ranch with her.

"You don't need to go," Norah insisted. "I can find my way all right."

"I want to check and see if the telephone is working," Mason insisted.

He knew it wasn't necessary for him to go with her, but he still had the impression that she didn't want to stay at the Bar 8 ranch. For the last hour of their return drive from Valentine, Norah had hardly talked at all, nor did she pay much attention to the scenery, although she'd been vibrant and enthusiastic earlier in the day. Perhaps she was only tired, but he sensed there was more to it than that.

Mason was impelled to see Norah settled safely for the night. He went into the house with her, checked the phone and found that it still wasn't in service.

"You have my cell phone, so you can telephone if you need to," he said. She looked rather forlorn standing in the middle of the big dining room, and he said, "Are you sure you're all right?"

"I'm ashamed to admit this, but I know it's going to get dark soon, and I'm afraid. I've always lived in the city, where it never gets dark. Just telling you about it makes me realize how foolish I sound. I'm determined to stay here. I *will* be all right," she said as if she was trying to convince herself.

"There's a security light in the yard. It won't be completely dark, and you can leave lights on in the house. But you're welcome to stay at the Flying K until you adjust to being in the country."

Forcing a smile, Norah said, "You have work to

do, so go back to the ranch and don't worry about me. I agreed to do this job, and I'm going to stay here alone tonight if it kills me. If I ever go to work on the mission field, I'll probably spend many nights alone.''

Mason was becoming fond of Norah, perhaps too fond for his own good. It troubled him every time she mentioned her desire to become a missionary, because it seemed to drive an insurmountable wedge between them. Such a decision should be kept between Norah and God, and he was determined that he wouldn't interfere. Better to keep his emotions and thoughts to himself until Norah came to terms with her future.

"You'll be safe enough, and I can be here in a short time if you need me."

"You hired me to be a cook. It isn't your responsibility to be my guardian." She placed her hand on his shoulder, intending to lead him toward the door. She might as well have tried to move Mount Rushmore. He didn't budge until he was ready.

"Keep the cell phone handy, and let me know if you're uneasy." He looked at her keenly, a sense of wonderment in his eyes. "I've had a great day."

"So did I, Mason. It's a day I'll never forget."

Chapter Five

The Bar 8 ranch house seemed as quiet as a tomb after Mason left, but with dogged determination, Norah stored her groceries in the cabinets and refrigerators and made a Caesar salad. The large dining room intimidated her, and she sat on a stool at the long work island in the center of the kitchen to eat her meal. Instead of thinking about the silence around her, she forced herself to concentrate on the day she'd spent with Mason.

She'd enjoyed the beautiful scenery, so different from her Missouri countryside, but more than that, it had been pleasant to be in Mason's company. Until today, she hadn't realized how satisfying male company could be. Mason was a good companion, and for a moment, she contemplated what it would be like to spend the rest of her life with someone like him. At that point, she stopped her speculation. When she was younger, Norah had looked forward to marriage, but always with a man who shared her interest in overseas missions. Mason King wasn't that man, and she had to discourage any flights of fancy about lifelong companionship with him.

Norah washed the few dishes by hand rather than use the large dishwasher. She locked every door and window on the first floor and turned out all the lights except the one on the front porch. She dropped Mason's cell phone in her pocket and went upstairs to settle in, closing all the draperies on the second floor.

The four bedrooms were equal in size, so Norah had chosen the one with a view of the rangeland. The rooms were sparsely furnished. To make the room more like her crowded bedroom at home, she moved a platform rocker and footstool in from another room.

Mason had hooked up her television on a low table, and she angled the screen so she could watch from the bed or from the rocker. She laid her Bible on the bedside table and placed her crochet bag by the chair. For years, Norah had been making scarves and mittens for unfortunate children in the United States and overseas. Her current project was crocheting cardigans for newborns of low-income single mothers.

Tonight Norah wasn't in the mood for crocheting or television, and she picked up the Bible. Soon she would have to search for Scriptural guidance to deal with her conflicting emotions about Mason, but tonight she had to come to grips with her fear of darkness.

It wasn't difficult to figure out what had caused her fears. Her own mother had been afraid of darkness due to a frightening childhood experience. It had never been completely dark in the Williamson household, because streetlights were numerous. On the occasions when a power outage occurred, her mother had chased away the darkness with candles and lamplight. Norah's siblings had mastered their phobias when they left home for college, and Norah was determined that she would, too.

The Bible was Norah's guide for all situations, and she checked out references to darkness. She didn't want to talk to herself, but reading Scripture out loud would be an antidote to her fear, so she read in a strong voice, "'You, O Lord, keep my lamp burning; my God turns my darkness into light.'" The sound of her voice did make the silence more bearable.

David, king of Israel, had written those words when he was praising God for victory over his enemies. David believed that, with God's help, he could overcome any obstacle. If David was that confident in the power of God, surely Norah could use that same faith and power to banish her own particular problem.

When she further read aloud the words of Jesus, "'I am the light of the world. Whoever follows me will never walk in darkness, but will have the light of life,'" Norah knew that unreasonable fear was inconsistent with her Christian faith. Remembering other hurdles God had helped her conquer gave Norah courage to trust Him to sustain her on the Bar 8 ranch through the night.

Norah laid aside the Bible, but in spite of all the Scriptural assurances she'd read, as she prepared for bed, the quietness and darkness were still intimidating. Who would ever have thought that she would long for the sound of a car driving by? Or the racket of the CDs her young neighbor played at deafening tones? She pulled open the draperies and opened the window, but she heard nothing except a cow bawling in the distance. What a difference a few days had made in her environment! The tomblike silence was so penetrating that she jumped when the phone rang.

"Just checking to see if you were all right before I hit the hay," Mason said when she picked up the phone.

"All locked in nice and tight," she answered, a lilt in her voice. "I've been reading the Bible, trying to put my hang-ups about nighttime to rest. It's working. I'll be fine in a day or two. I'm slow to adjust to new situations."

"What are you planning for tomorrow?"

"I intend to call the offices of H & H and learn what their schedule will be and what they expect of me. After that, I'll start planning menus."

"Sounds like a dull day to me," he said, chuckling. "I have an idea to help you overcome your fear of the night."

"What is it?" she said hesitantly.

"There'll be a full moon tomorrow night. I'd like to take you to a place without any light except the moon and the stars. The beauty of the night will be so wonderful, you won't think about being afraid. How does that sound?"

It sounded as if she would be putting a lot of confidence in Mason King if she went with him into an unknown area surrounded by darkness.

But instead of voicing her doubts, Norah said, "Interesting. Sort of like a therapy session, huh?"

"Maybe. I'll build a campfire and cook our meal just like the old-timers used to do it. We'll go on horseback."

A silence greeted his remark. "Uh…" Norah stalled. "I don't know."

"You don't know what?"

"There's one little hitch in your plan. I've never ridden a horse."

"Never ridden a horse!"

Norah stifled a hoot of laughter. Mason's shock was as great as it might have been if she'd admitted she'd never brushed her teeth.

Mason had been given his own pony when he was five years old, and he'd ridden behind his father for as long as he could remember. Hardly believing he'd heard her correctly, he asked, "You aren't afraid of horses, too?"

His agitation amused Norah, and she could no longer restrain her laughter as she teased, "No. I'm just a city greenhorn."

"We could take the truck, but that would spoil the atmosphere," Mason offered, and Norah sensed his disappointment.

"If you have some old nag that won't pitch me off, I'm willing to try. There's not much to riding, is there?"

Mason knew he had a problem on his hands, but he said patiently, "There's a *lot* to riding, and I can't teach you riding skills in one evening. But you come prepared to ride, and we'll manage. It will be a short ride."

"Deal! What time do you want me to come?"

"About six o'clock. We'll ride to our destination,

cook the meal and let the darkness close in around us. You'll enjoy it.''

''Well…maybe. At least I'm game to try it. Thanks, Mason.'' She hung up.

Norah turned out the light and stretched full-length under the blanket. Her heart was singing. She no longer felt afraid, for she knew Mason was as close as the telephone. And God was close, too. Norah turned on her side, facing the opaqueness outside her window, repeating the words of the Psalmist. '''At night His song shall be with me.'''

Gradually, Norah realized that the room was flooded with moonlight. From her bed, she saw the moon hovering above the Bar 8, signifying that the God of creation was very near.

Using the toll-free number Sheila gave her, Norah telephoned the H & H offices the next afternoon. She had a helpful conversation with Jim Hanson, the athletic director of the therapy program, who would be staying at the Bar 8 ranch throughout the summer.

Jim told her there would be three four-week sessions, the first one to start the first week in June, the last one ending the last week in August, with a week-long break for the Fourth of July. There would be approximately six children each session, with an average of two or more volunteers for each rider.

In addition to Jim, a nurse, Carolyn Turner, would be a full-time employee. The other workers would be unpaid volunteers, some for the whole summer, others a few weeks at a time. Each session would deal with three different types of disabilities—one for blind children, one for the physically impaired, the other for children with mental disabilities. Two children would be housed together in a room with one adult volunteer.

"Since this is a pilot program," Jim explained, "we'll be learning as we go."

Norah would be expected to provide three meals each day for at least twenty people. Breakfast would be served at eight o'clock, lunch at noon and dinner at six o'clock in the evening. Norah's wages were included in the fee H & H paid Mason for use of his ranch facilities and horses. But the organization would issue vouchers for the groceries, pay the utilities and hire Sheila to help in the kitchen and dining room. The children would go home on weekends, leaving Friday afternoon and returning on Monday morning.

"But as I mentioned," Jim said, "this is a new undertaking for all of us, so I hope you can adapt your schedule as we find it necessary."

"I'll do my best," Norah said, "but I've never cooked for so many people over an extended period. The first weeks will be experimental for me, too."

"I'm sure we'll get along fine," Jim said. "Hopefully, the program will be so successful that the project will be funded for many years to come. Our long-range goal is to expand the program to include adults with disabilities, too."

"Whew!" Norah said aloud when she finished the conversation. It sounded like a busy summer, but she welcomed the tight schedule. Providing three meals each day, starting to cook before six o'clock and finishing only in time to go to bed and start the same schedule over again, would hopefully get her mind off Mason.

Thoughts of Mason had a tendency to disrupt the work she'd come to Nebraska to do. When she tried to plan menus for the H & H children, she found herself staring into space thinking of Mason. His winning smile, his compassionate nature and his captivating presence had dominated her dreams and trespassed on her daytime hours. It had to stop!

Determined to exert more self-control, Norah carried her box of recipe books into the kitchen and placed them on a convenient shelf near the stove. She needed to plan and buy supplies for at least two weeks. It wouldn't be easy cooking meals to suit both children and adults. Jim had told her that, for this first session, they had chosen children without dietary limitations so she wouldn't need to be concerned about providing special dishes. Although the first four weeks would tend to be trial and error, once she had those meals planned, she could use the same menus for the next two sessions.

As she spent the afternoon planning, she tried to remember the foods her siblings liked when they were younger. Thinking about them saddened her. Not only had she lost her father and disabled brother, she'd lost the others, too.

While her father lived, she'd gone overboard to maintain harmony in the family. Even when she believed her siblings were imposing on her, she took it with a smile because she didn't want to disturb her father. But now she was alienated from her remaining family.

The family property had been willed to her without any strings, but had she been wrong to put the home up for sale? Had Sam been right when he'd told her that their father had intended for her to keep it intact for the family to use? If that was so, why hadn't her father told her that, or at least provided sufficient funds for its upkeep?

She'd received a monthly compensation from her father for the housekeeping duties, but upon his death, that income had ceased. The house was old and large, and in constant need of repairs. If she kept the property, her meager savings would soon be depleted.

Besides, she wanted a new life. If she couldn't

become an overseas missionary at this late date, she hoped for a profession of some kind rather than spending her senior years as an unpaid baby-sitter for her nieces and nephews.

It disturbed Norah that she hadn't apologized to her brother and sisters, but how could she when she didn't believe she had been unfair to them? She did remember that Jesus had told His followers if anyone had been treated unjustly, the one who had been wronged should initiate reconciliation. Perhaps she would do that, but her emotional pain was too raw right now to make the first move.

But she felt completely cut off from her previous life. Was that the reason she'd taken to Mason so quickly? Maybe at the end of the summer, she would contact her siblings and ask forgiveness, but in the meantime, she would spend her time ministering to children whose problems were certainly worse than hers. She prayed that in helping others, she would also find healing.

By five o'clock, she laid her books and schedules aside and prepared for her get-together with Mason. She'd noticed that the temperature dropped quickly as soon as the sun set, so she put on a heavy pair of jeans, and a blouse with a sweatshirt over it. She wore woolen socks under a pair of leather boots.

She debated over what to wear on her head, but finally decided on a narrow-brimmed hat that she'd worn when she worked in the flower gardens. She tied a scarf around her neck, which might come in handy if the wind was too strong to wear the hat. With a lot of anticipation, and some apprehension, she set out for the Flying K ranch.

Chapter Six

Mason wasn't in sight when Norah reached the Flying K, but a burro was tied to the hitching post in front of the house. A metal tripod, gridiron and bulging saddlebags were secured to the burro's harness. Deciding Mason must be preparing for their outing, Norah sat on the porch and enjoyed the song of the meadowlark that warbled lustily from his perch on a fence post. A grayish-brown prairie hen led her small brood of chicks across the yard, teaching them by example how to feed on the insects and plants.

Mason was obviously a good steward of his property, for the buildings were painted, the ground was free of debris and the fences were intact and sturdy. The fence around the corral interested Norah, for on each post, there was a worn-out pair of cowboy boots. Buster, the bull, grazed inside the corral, and once he looked toward her and bawled.

"Don't bawl at me," she said in mock severity. "I'm still mad at you for causing me to wreck my car."

Chewing on a juicy morsel of grass, Buster bawled again, long and loud, and Norah's mouth curved into a smile. She would never forget Buster's welcome to the Flying K.

Soon Mason emerged from the barn, leading two saddled horses, and Norah eyed the animals warily as he approached.

"Ready?" he said, a wide smile breaking across his bearded face. He tugged on Norah's hand, encouraging her off the porch.

"I'm not sure," Norah said uneasily.

Mason told her that her mount would be the small palomino with a golden coat and silvery mane and tail. He would ride the brownish quarter horse. As Mason spoke fondly of the two horses, and detailed their capabilities, Norah reached out a tentative hand and stroked the palomino's flanks.

"You have nothing to be afraid of," Mason promised her. "I've been weeding out my tamest mounts and taking them to the Bar 8, and following instructions from the H & H, Doug has been exercising them for the children when they come. But the palomino is gentle, too.''

''I've learned all of my ranch lore from Wild West movies,'' Norah said nervously, ''where the horses all seem to be bronco-busting animals. And where city slickers are sometimes given a bucking horse to test their mettle.'' She turned solemn blue eyes toward Mason.

''I wouldn't put you on an animal like that,'' Mason assured her. He was eager to introduce Norah to his way of life in a manner that would make her love it as much as he did.

Recognizing his sincerity, Norah touched his forearm. ''I know you wouldn't, Mason. I was joking with you. I'm a slow learner, but be patient with me, and I'll soon catch on.''

Mason assessed her clothes. ''It might have been wise for you to bring a coat, but I have a couple of blankets on the burro if it cools down.''

He wore a blue flannel shirt, heavy blue jeans and a suede vest, looking every bit the cowboy of a century ago.

Mason motioned her toward the horses, and put his hand on the mane of the palomino. ''This is Daisy,'' he said. ''If you like her, she can be your personal mount while you're here.''

When the mare turned soulful, liquid eyes in her direction, Norah felt as if she'd made a new friend.

Mason lifted the bridle. "This serves the same purpose as the steering wheel on your car. The metal part of the bridle, called a bit, fits in the horse's mouth. The reins, these long, narrow leather strips, are attached to the bit. If you want the horse to turn left, you gently pull the reins in that direction, and so on. But tonight, don't be concerned about that. Just concentrate on staying on the horse. Daisy will follow me."

Norah touched Daisy's long nose, and the mare tried to nuzzle her fingers.

"She likes apples," Mason said. He took a red apple from his pocket and extended it toward Daisy. She mouthed the apple and started chewing.

"Always mount a horse from the left side," Mason continued, illustrating as he talked. "Take the reins and the horse's mane in your left hand and put your left foot in the stirrup." He indicated a wooden, flat-bottomed ring. "With your right hand grab the back of the saddle. Spring up, swing your right leg over the horse's rump and switch your right hand to the pommel of the saddle here in the center. Sit easily in the saddle and put your right foot in the stirrup."

He mounted the horse with a swift, graceful movement. The blood rushed to Norah's face, and she gasped in admiration of his powerful body.

Dismounting, Mason looked at Norah quickly, apparently thinking his instructions had caused her confusion, for he hastily said, "It takes practice to give you self-confidence, so I'll help you this time. Eventually, horseback riding becomes as natural as breathing, and you won't even think about what you're doing. Lift your left foot to the stirrup, and I'll boost you into the saddle. Ready?"

It seemed like a long stretch to the stirrup, but when she managed to reach it, Mason put his hands around her waist and smoothly lifted her into the saddle. His touch was electrifying! The warmth of his hands seemed to sear her flesh through the heavy layers of clothing. She wished she wasn't so sensitive to Mason's masculine appeal. She excused her reaction by reasoning that she hadn't been exposed to much male company, especially to a man as vibrant as Mason.

She tucked her foot into the other stirrup, as if she'd been riding horses all of her life. But when she picked up the reins, and looked down at Mason, it seemed a long way to the ground.

Mason watched her with something akin to awe. How could she have gladdened his heart so much in a few days? If she'd perked up his life already, what effect would she have on him after three months of seeing her almost every day? But regardless of the consequences, he couldn't remember when he'd ever anticipated a summer with more gladness of heart.

Mason checked the stirrups to be sure they were adjusted for Norah's legs. "Are you comfortable?"

"Not very," she said with a laugh, "but it's more emotional than physical."

"Ride beside me, and if you have any problem, say so."

He hooked the leading string of the burro to his saddle and mounted his horse with agility and ease.

Again, Norah admired his graceful movements, wondering if she'd ever be that confident on a horse.

"Hold your reins loosely and let Daisy take care of you," he instructed. "Don't sit so rigid. Relax, and let your body move with the horse. Before your duties start with H & H, I'll teach you how to saddle Daisy and how to care for her."

"Seems like there's a lot to horseback riding," Norah said ruefully.

"If you ride every day, you'll soon learn."

"But I won't have time to ride every day." As the horses moved forward, she told him what she'd learned from the Omaha office. "I've already started preparations."

The wind ruffled the manes of the horses, and Norah's hat blew off before they were out of sight of the ranch buildings. Mason jumped off his horse to retrieve the hat. He sprinted after it, but when he stooped to pick it up, a stronger gust of wind boosted it several yards beyond him. When it landed in a small lake, Norah called, "Don't bother with it. It's an old hat."

Thankful she'd thought to bring the scarf, Norah wound it around her head.

"That wasn't much of a hat for a range woman anyway," Mason said when he was in the saddle again.

"Is the wind always like this?" she asked.

"No. Most of the time it's a lot stronger."

Norah glanced at him, and she knew he wasn't joking. She'd need to buy a hat that tied under the chin like the one Mason wore.

They rode through waving grass that brushed the horses' bellies. On the half-hour ride, Norah enjoyed seeing the prairie at close range. The velocity of the wind blew the grass in surging green waves, and it was easy to believe that they were riding on the ocean. She understood why Mason preferred to ride a horse, for this was an easier way to enjoy the serenity of the grasslands than by riding in a vehicle.

The wind swept the words from her mouth as she called, "Why is this area called the Sand Hills?"

"In prehistoric times, the smooth contours of the prairie were made by sand transported here by the wind. Then grasses took root. We don't get much rainfall, but there are vast deposits of water in the porous rocks beneath the surface.''

He motioned to a water tank, with a windmill towering over it. ''We have lots of water if we dig for it, and with so much wind, we have a constant supply of water for our cattle.''

Mason had been watching Norah closely, and near the end of the ride, he asked, ''Getting tired?''

''My legs are kinda numb, and my back hurts.''

''You're sitting too stiff, but you'll soon get over that. Blend your body into the horse's movements. It won't be much longer. We stop at the next coulee, where we'll be out of sight of the security light at ranch headquarters. I want it to be completely dark when the moon comes up.''

''I saw the moon from my window at the Bar 8 last night. Living in a city, I didn't often see the moon. It was a wonderful sight.''

''Wait until you see the moon rise tonight, and you'll really be impressed!''

The coulee was bisected by a small stream, with numerous plum bushes on its banks. A few plum blossoms remained, giving the area a sweet, spicy scent.

''We'll have our supper down here where it's not so windy, but we'll go to the crest of the hill when we look at the stars. The breeze calms down after dark.''

"What can I do to help?"

"Not a thing. You're my guest tonight." He loosened the horses' reins and staked them several yards from their campsite. Norah sat on the ground and watched in admiration as Mason prepared their meal. He built two fires. Over one, he set a tripod, opened a large can of baked beans, poured them into a smoke-covered pot and hung it over the flames.

He set a gridiron over the second fire, on which he arranged two thin-sliced steaks and placed a coffeepot directly in the coals.

"Do you cook like this often?"

"No, but my friends and I camp out when we go on hunting and fishing trips. It's a satisfying feeling to catch a large trout and have it frying in the pan in less than an hour. I suppose you don't fish, either?"

She shook her head negatively, but her eyes glowed with mirth. "Sorry I'm such a disappointment to you. Remember, I only gave you my credentials as a cook. I can cook and do fine needlework. Not much else."

"Oh, that's okay," he hastened to assure her. "I wanted to find out how I can entertain you this summer. Since you have weekends off, I want to show you around this part of the country."

"I learned today that I'll have the first week of July free, too, so I can help with the gathering at your ranch in July." She stood awkwardly. "I'm going to walk while you finish. My legs are stiff from riding."

"Don't go far. The food is almost ready. Besides, there are rattlesnakes in some of these canyons."

She stopped abruptly. "You've said the magic word—*snake*. I've decided I don't need a walk." She did a few simple stretching exercises to loosen her muscles until Mason said the food was ready.

The campfire had laced the meat with a pungent, smoky taste, and Norah commented to Mason that she'd never tasted any food that was more satisfying. "So you've introduced me to another new experience. Thanks."

His smile sent her pulses racing. "We'll plan other cookouts before the summer is over."

He produced slices of carrot cake from the saddlebags, and when Norah took her first bite, she said, "This didn't come from a deli!"

"You're right, but I didn't make it, either. Sheila's mother bakes cakes and pies for me occasionally, and she wraps portions for the freezer. I took this from the freezer this afternoon."

"You have good neighbors."

"Sure do. Settlers in the Sand Hills depended on their neighbors, and it's become our way of life. That's one thing that hasn't changed since my great-grandfather homesteaded here," Mason reminisced as they ate. "In the early days, everybody avoided the Sand Hills because there weren't many trees, not much rainfall and anyone who tried to farm this land failed. But my ancestor brought a herd of cattle from Texas and turned them loose to graze on the lush grass. They multiplied. When it was discovered that there was so much water underground, and that all you had to do was dig a well and put up a windmill, my father started irrigating. With the hay and grain we raise now, ranching is more profitable and much less risky than it once was."

Norah relaxed, listening to the soft tone of Mason's voice. A pair of ducks flew overhead, probably heading for the small pond that had claimed her hat.

"The Kings haven't been very prolific," he continued in a pensive tone. "My father was the only child of my grandparents who lived to adulthood. I'm an only child, and now that I have no children, the King line has about run out. I don't know what will happen to the ranch when I die."

"Pardon me for being nosy, but why haven't you married?" She almost gasped at her own audacity. Her face flushed, but Mason didn't seem to notice.

She thought that he was everything any woman could want, and was shocked to realize how many of her waking hours were spent thinking about Mason. Why was she so sensitive to this man's masculine appeal? Again, she wondered if Sam had characterized her correctly when he'd dubbed her a foolish old maid.

She received another shock when Mason said, "I was married, but it isn't a period of my life I like to talk about."

"Oh, I'm sorry I asked. Please forgive me." She was surprised at the raw, naked pain reflected on his face.

"No, it's all right, Norah," he said slowly as he stood and scattered the coals of the fire. "I want you to know, but we'll talk about it another time. Right now, I need to pack the equipment so we can reach the hill before it's dark. I want you to experience the full pleasure of having night fall around you."

"I'll help with the cleanup," she said hurriedly, embarrassed at bringing up a part of his past that disturbed him.

"Bring a bucket of water from the creek to douse the fire while I clean our utensils. Also, pick up any paper that might have blown away."

When Mason helped Norah back into the saddle, she was aware of some chafed, sore places on her legs and posterior, but she was determined that Mason wouldn't know anything about her discomfort. The trail out of the coulee was steep, and Norah clutched the reins, fearing she might fall backward. But Daisy kept her footing, following Mason and the burro, until they reached the top of the hill.

Once they dismounted, Mason spread a blanket on the ground and handed another one to Norah. "Wrap this around you if you get cold."

He brought the saddles and placed them on the blanket. "We may be here a few hours, and saddles make good backrests. I often use mine for a pillow when I camp overnight."

They'd stopped beside a blowout, a deep hole in the earth created by the wind. The blowout had little vegetation, but it was surrounded by grass which was more than two feet tall. The breeze was brisk, and before she sat down, Norah wrapped the extra blanket around her shoulders. She leaned her back against the saddle that still retained the warmth of the horse.

Mason and the horses were only dim outlines in the fast-approaching darkness. When he sat beside her, she found it difficult to make out his features. He stretched out on the blanket and put his head on the saddle. Even with Mason nearby, Norah was fearful and overwhelmed by the darkness—a darkness so thick, it could be felt.

"Look up!" Mason said.

The last time she'd looked at the sky, it had been darkish and obscure. Now the obscurity had disappeared, and the stars were visible, sparkling like diamonds across the heavens.

"How beautiful!" Norah whispered into a sound-less universe.

"It's awesome!" Mason agreed. "When I'm out on a night like this, I'm overwhelmed by the majesty of God. It's awesome," he repeated. "The Psalmist said that God knows the number of the stars. With our limited vision, we only see a portion of the heavens, and I can't even count those stars, yet God knows how many there are in the whole universe. Do you see the Big Dipper?"

Norah shook her head, but realizing he couldn't see the gesture, she said, "No."

"I want you to see it before the moon comes up, which is going to happen soon. We're facing east—you can see the glow of the moon. Look to your left, which is north." He found her hand in the darkness, and pointed her toward the constellation. "There are seven stars in the Big Dipper, and the two stars in the front of the cup point to the North Star. Lots of nights, I've found my way home by watching the North Star."

"Oh, yes, I see it," Norah cried excitedly. "It looks just like the pictures in my elementary school science books. And there's the Little Dipper! The North Star is at the end of the Little Dipper's handle. This is exciting!"

"'The heavens declare the glory of God; and the

skies proclaim the work of His hands,'" Mason softly quoted one of his favorite Bible verses.

"I've known that Scripture for years, but it takes on new meaning in a setting like this."

The darkness intensified, and Norah held up her hand. "I've always heard of darkness so deep you couldn't see your hand in front of your face, but I didn't believe it until now. Thanks for arranging this experience, Mason. It will help me master my fear of the night."

He took her hand, and slowly the darkness receded as a brilliant glow appeared in the eastern sky and a sliver of moon peeped over the horizon. The radiance increased until the sky was flooded with light, and the stars could hardly be seen at all.

Norah felt as if she were in a holy place, such as the one Moses had experienced when God had told him to take off his shoes because he was standing on holy ground. With the glory of God displayed around her, she felt small and insignificant.

It was a time for silence, but she was so overcome by the majesty of the night that she softly quoted the words from another of David's psalms.

"'When I consider your heavens, the work of your fingers, the moon and the stars, which You have set in place, what is man that You are mindful of him, the son of man that You care for him?'"

Mason squeezed her hand. "I'd intended to talk

with you about my marriage tonight, but somehow this doesn't seem to be the time nor the place. Do you mind?''

''Not at all,'' Norah assured him. Tonight it seemed as if she and Mason were alone in the universe, and she liked it that way. It would spoil the pleasure of the night to hear about a time when Mason had belonged to another woman.

Chapter Seven

They didn't return to the Flying K until two o'clock in the morning, and Norah was so stiff and sore that Mason had to lift her from the saddle.

"Sorry I kept you out so late," Mason said contritely. "I always get carried away when I'm out on a night like this, and I forget what time it is."

The full moon cast its glimmering shadows over them, and Mason's face, with his heavy whiskers and deep-set eyes, was mysterious and unreadable. But she discerned a half smile of affection playing across his mouth, and Norah's fingers softly caressed his bearded cheek.

"Don't apologize. I've never had a more wonderful time. I feel closer to God right now than I ever have in my life. I enjoyed the opportunity to appreciate the majesty of God and the wonders of His universe as we did tonight. Our time together gave me the courage I need to tackle my work this summer and make some difficult decisions about my future.''

Norah started toward her car, walking as stiff-legged as a killdeer, and Mason said, ''I'll follow you to the Bar 8 to be sure you get there all right.''

''That isn't necessary. I'll be okay.''

''But I aim to make sure of it.'' He tied the horses and burro to the hitching post. ''It won't hurt the animals to stand here until I get back. They've been munching on fresh new grass all evening.''

Norah didn't protest further. She wasn't sure she could keep her eyes open until she reached her destination, and it was a very comforting to see the steady headlights of Mason's truck following.

At the Bar 8, he walked up on the porch with her and waited until he heard the lock turn before he went back to the pickup. A light came on in an upstairs bedroom, and Norah stepped in front of the window and waved. Mason tooted the horn, and with a satisfied smile on his face, headed toward the Flying K.

He hadn't mentioned his marriage to anyone for years. Why did it suddenly seem so important to tell Norah about the time he'd lost both his wife and son? Would it be presumptuous to tell her why he wouldn't take the risk of loving and marrying again?

Norah had intended to sleep late, but aching muscles brought her awake soon after daylight. From the waist down, there wasn't a spot on her body that didn't hurt. As determined as she was to become a part of Mason's world, she doubted she'd ever swing her leg over another saddle.

A hot soaking bath eased a lot of the discomfort, but she still waddled like a duck when she went downstairs for breakfast. The memories of the beautiful evening remained in Norah's mind all day as she planned menus and organized the kitchen to make it more convenient. Sheila came in the afternoon and helped to unpack and organize all the cooking pans, dishes, glassware and silver that they'd use during the summer.

At the end of the day, Norah went to the screened-in porch that held a half-dozen padded rocking chairs, a few low tables and a wooden swing. She was resting, drinking lemonade when Mason drove into the driveway.

Mason climbed the two steps, opened the screen door and sat down in a massive wooden rocker. He'd apparently had a hard day, too, for he sighed and stretched out his long legs. "Must be nice to have nothing to do but sit around on the porch."

"Careful!" she said. "After what I've been doing today, those are fighting words."

"Been busy, huh?"

"Yes, and I'm tired to the bone, but it's a good feeling when I consider how much I've accomplished. Sheila and I have the kitchen ready for use, and we're going shopping tomorrow. H & H headquarters e-mailed her today that they'd faxed some vouchers to the grocery store in Valentine. Now that I'm almost ready for them, I'm getting excited about the kids coming."

Mason shuffled his feet. "If you're not too tired to listen, I came to finish a conversation we started last night."

"My ears aren't tired—just the rest of my body. I'll bring you a glass of lemonade, and then we can talk."

She lifted her body gingerly from the chair and limped toward the inside door.

Watching her slow progress, Mason commented, "I figured you'd be a little uncomfortable today. I'll bring Daisy to the Bar 8, so you can ride every day. It'll take a while, but the way to get rid of the soreness is to ride consistently."

Norah didn't comment. She didn't want him to know how discouraged she was by the effect the ride had on her. She poured lemonade over a glass of ice, put some cookies on a plate and placed them on a table by his chair.

Looking over the fields, Mason twirled the glass in his hand, still having trouble putting his past into words. Finally he turned to face her. "I married when I was nineteen, and my wife was a year younger. We'd been in love with each other since we were kids. One month before our first wedding anniversary, she gave birth to a stillborn son and died a few hours later."

"Oh, I'm so sorry."

He acknowledged her sympathy with a nod. "I thought my life was over, but Dad, who'd also lost a young wife, knew how I felt. He thought I should get away from the Flying K for a while, so he encouraged me to go to college. I went to the University of Nebraska and graduated with a degree in agriculture. I was only twenty-five, and still had a life ahead of me, but I felt empty. However, I came back home and settled down to help Dad operate the ranch. We had several good years before he died."

There were many questions that Norah wanted to ask. Why hadn't he married again? Was he still mourning the loss of his wife? It seemed inconceivable to her that anyone would mourn so long, but she remained silent, waiting for Mason to continue at his own pace.

"Dad encouraged me to marry again and have a

family. I dated a few women, but I always stopped short of asking anyone to marry me.''

''You didn't love any of them?''

''I reckon that was it, but they were perfectly fine women, and I probably could have learned to love again. No, it went deeper than that. I was afraid to get married.''

''Afraid!''

''Not of getting married, but afraid of fathering another child. You see, I blame myself for my wife's death. She was reluctant to get pregnant, but I wanted children to inherit the Flying K, and I finally persuaded her to have a baby. If I hadn't done that, she'd be alive today.''

Norah hardly knew what to say, but he paused and looked at her, as if waiting for a comment.

''She might have lost the child even if you'd waited several years. But that still doesn't explain why you haven't married again.''

''Because,'' he said, without meeting her eyes, ''I wouldn't risk another woman's life to bring my children into the world.''

''There have been so many improvements in prenatal care and obstetrics that it's rare for a woman to die in childbirth. In fact, it was unusual even when your wife died.''

''She had a rare blood disease that caused her problem.''

"So she would probably have had complications at any age."

As if he hadn't heard her, Mason said, "I kept thinking I would marry, but just didn't get around to it. Finally, five years ago, I decided I was too old to take on the responsibilities of a child. A middle-aged man doesn't have the strength and energy to keep up with a teenage kid. I didn't want to be a senior citizen when my son went to college. I figured I'd make a lousy father."

"Having never been married myself, I'm a poor one to comment, but there are other reasons for marriage besides bearing children. In fact, *love* is the only reason for people to marry. Having children is a by-product of their love."

Mason didn't seem to pay attention to her observation. "I wanted you to know about my unpleasant experience with marriage," he said, with obvious relief that he'd told her what she needed to know. Changing the subject abruptly, he continued, "Did you sleep last night?"

"Yes. I was so tired when I went to bed that I forgot about the darkness. I know it's childish to panic at the thought of living alone, but my life has always been stable, doing the same things week after week. I stayed in our family home alone for a few months after my father died, but I didn't like it.

That's one reason I put the house on the market. But I'll soon adjust to living by myself.''

''So when do your duties start?''

''The children will be coming soon, but several staff members will move in next Friday.''

''There are so many places I want to take you this summer.''

''I'm supposed to have weekends free, but that depends on my work schedule. I may have to spend some weekends preparing for the next week.''

''Then what shall we do this weekend?''

''Why not come tomorrow evening for supper? I've invited Sheila and Doug. There's a gas grill on the back porch that I want to try before our guests arrive. That grove of cottonwood trees behind the house looks like it would make a good area for the children to have occasional cookouts. I'll try it out on you and the Johnsons first.''

''What time?''

''Whenever you and Doug finish your work.''

''I'll try to be here by half-past six. I'll ride over and bring Daisy. We'll spend some of your free time on riding lessons.''

Early the next morning, Sheila and Norah set out for Valentine, Sheila driving a truck and Norah following in her car, which she intended to leave at the garage for repairs. They spent a busy morning buying supplies, lunched at a small diner and returned to the Bar 8 by midafternoon.

Norah delighted in Sheila's company. The young woman was intelligent, witty and helpful, and Norah found herself wishing she could have enjoyed such camaraderie with her sisters. The age difference between her and Sheila wasn't a barrier, but her sisters always seemed to think that Norah was ancient and wouldn't understand their thoughts and needs. As she often did, Norah wondered what she could have done to develop a better relationship with her siblings. Shaking herself mentally, she decided to forget the past, which she couldn't change, and concentrate on the future.

"I'll make potato salad for our supper," Sheila volunteered when they'd gotten all the supplies stored in the kitchen cabinets. Impulsively, Sheila put her arms around Norah and hugged her tightly.

"It's going to be fun having you here the rest of the summer," Sheila continued. "We so rarely have anyone new come to the community that it gets kinda boring. Now, not only you, but all the H & H people will be here for several months to liven things up."

Norah was touched by Sheila's sincerity and welcome. The Williamsons had never been an affectionate family, and this natural gesture of Sheila's brought a mist of tears to Norah's eyes.

"I don't know how lively I'll be," Norah said. "I just hope I can keep up with the fast pace."

After Sheila left, Norah made a pie from the fresh peaches she'd bought at the supermarket. Then she filled a casserole with scalloped mixed vegetables and put it in the oven. The rest of the meal would be simple—hamburger patties and buns.

At six o'clock, Mason rode around the house into the grove of trees where Norah was putting hamburgers on the grill. He was astride his favorite quarter horse and leading the palomino Norah had ridden.

"I'll turn Daisy into the corral, and maybe tomorrow evening I can teach you how to saddle and care for her."

"I doubt you can do that in one evening. Remember, I'm a slow learner," she said, laughing up at him.

Mason's gaze was fixed on her face, and he drew a deep breath as he sensed the undeniable attraction building between them. A magnetism so powerful that he wondered if he had the strength to keep this woman at arm's length all summer. He had to keep reminding himself that his own hang-ups about marriage, as well as her desire to become a missionary, hindered any serious relationship between them. He could never fit into her world, and he doubted she would accept his.

Mason desperately wished that God would reveal the future so he might know what move to make. But Mason had learned long ago that God expected His followers to live by faith. Mason lifted the reins and rode toward the corral without speaking.

Norah stared after Mason in bewilderment before she turned toward the picnic area. What had caused the confusion and uncertainty on his face? And she wished she wasn't so conscious of Mason's magnetic personality. His mere presence had the power to send her spirits soaring. She both anticipated and dreaded the next few months when she could expect to see Mason at any time.

Mason returned about the time Doug and Sheila arrived. Doug had a guitar slung over his shoulder, and he said, "Thought we could have some dinner music."

"You call what you do to that guitar music?" Mason jeered good-naturedly.

"Norah can be the judge," Doug retorted in kind. "She's probably a connoisseur of fine music."

"No music until after we've eaten," Sheila said. Lifting the lid of the grill, she added, "These burgers are ready. Do you want Mason to say the blessing?" she asked Norah.

"Yes, please."

Mason and Doug took off their hats while Mason prayed in simple terms, asking God's blessing on their food. There was nothing showy about Mason's faith, but Norah sensed that he had a deep, abiding Christian belief in the majesty and the goodness of God. A faith that had guided him through the difficult circumstances he'd encountered as a youth.

Listening to Doug and Mason talk about the rigors of ranching, Norah realized what a risky occupation these men followed. Their livelihood depended on the consistency of nature, so it was no wonder Mason had developed a keen dependence upon the providence of God.

After they'd eaten, Doug and Mason helped carry the food and utensils into the kitchen, then wandered to the front porch, cups of coffee in their hands. When Norah and Sheila joined them, Doug was strumming gently on the guitar. Sheila sat on a cushion near Doug's chair, and Norah went to the swing, where she swayed gently back and forth in time to the music. Mason took the cups to the kitchen and sat in a chair near the swing when he returned.

In a rich soprano, Sheila started singing softly, "O give me a home where the buffalo roam," and soon Doug's tenor, and Mason's deep bass joined Sheila's as they sang "Home on the Range," a favorite of Western music fans for generations. Norah hummed the music as they sang.

Norah applauded when they finished. "Your talent is impressive. You'd be a big hit in Nashville or Branson.''

Pretending embarrassment, Doug clowned. ''Aw, pshaw, ma'am, you're being too kind about our caterwauling.''

''I'm serious. Your harmony is amazing. Do you sing often?''

''Just once in a while like this,'' Mason said, ''but we might sing more often if we had a good alto, and you've got the voice for it. Start another song, Sheila, so Norah can sing with us.''

''I don't know a lot of songs,'' Norah said.

''You probably know 'Amazing Grace,''' Doug said.

When Norah nodded, he struck a chord and Norah's voice blended with the others in the words, ''Amazing grace, how sweet the sound.''

''Hey!'' Sheila said, clapping her hands at the end of the song. ''Maybe we *can* go to Nashville. I've always had a hankering to sing professionally.''

''Forget it,'' Mason said. ''I have a ranch to run.''

''At least, we should plan to entertain the H & H kids,'' Norah said. ''Let's have a Wild West party for each group, and we can provide the musical entertainment. I'm sure Jim Hanson would like it. He's concerned about having enough activities to keep the children occupied. Most of them are city kids, and he thinks they might find ranch country too quiet.''

''And there's no reason,'' Sheila said, ''that we can't practice and sing for the Fourth of July celebration. I'm on the entertainment committee, and I haven't found any singers yet. We can do Western favorites and hymns, and our neighbors would love it.''

''Maybe we *can* go on the road,'' Doug said. ''Singing groups are pretty scarce in this part of the state.''

''Don't get carried away, Doug,'' Mason said. ''I don't have time for that and neither do you. About the time we had a concert planned, our cows would start calving, or it would be time to put up hay.''

''We're not too busy in the winter, and that's when there's a call for entertainers,'' Sheila argued.

''Don't count on me,'' Norah said. ''I'll be leaving in September.''

''At least we can sing this summer,'' Sheila said, refusing to relinquish her plan. ''Let's practice and work up a repertoire for the kids and the Fourth of July.''

Doug and Norah enthusiastically agreed with her. Mason was more reluctant, but he finally said, ''I'm shorthanded for workers this summer, but if you'll use songs I already know, I'll help out.''

From her seat in the swing, Norah studied Mason's profile, and she wondered what he'd look like without whiskers. He was close enough that she could reach out and touch his arm—and her fingers tingled with the desire to do so. Mason looked in her direction and as his dark eyes met her blue ones, a spark ignited, confusing her emotions. His eyes searched her face, and she wondered if he could read her thoughts. Mason reached a hand toward her and hastily withdrew it, but a hint of wonder brightened his eyes before Norah looked away.

Sheila saw the gesture, and with a grin and up-lifted eyebrows, she glanced at her husband. Doug shook his head in warning. As he continued to strum the guitar strings softly, Norah and Mason experienced a mutual awareness, creating an unmistakable bond between them. For a warm, heady interlude, their hearts had composed a mutual song.

Chapter Eight

The first week with the children passed more quickly than Norah had dreamed that it would. As the two vans drove away from the Bar 8 on Friday afternoon, several little hands fluttered from the windows, waving goodbye. Norah's heart tightened as she thought about each of the children who'd participated in the first week of therapy.

The first three weeks of H & H activities were designed to train six children who were legally blind. They'd arrived at the ranch on Monday morning, accompanied by Seeing Eye dogs. There were fourteen volunteers, of various ages—the youngest, a boy of sixteen, the oldest, a seventy-five-year-old woman. It had been a week of learning for everyone.

When the last van left the Bar 8, Norah eased into

one of the rocking chairs on the porch. "It's been quite a week," she said to Jim Hanson, the therapist and athletic director of the H & H program, who leaned against a porch post.

"Yes, it has," Jim agreed. "Overall, what's your evaluation of the program?"

Jim was thirty-five, of medium height and muscular build. His blond hair and blue eyes suggested his Norwegian ancestry. He was easygoing, compassionate and an expert in his field.

Norah considered his question for a few minutes. "After only five days, I've seen improvement in most of the children. They have more confidence, and all were smiling today. There weren't many smiles the first day."

"Fear of the unknown," Jim said. "Most of these children had never been close to a horse before. For a day or two, they wouldn't even touch the animal. But this morning, all of the children mounted the horses and rode short distances around the inside arena."

Carolyn Turner, the petite, dark-haired resident nurse of the program, came out of the house carrying a medical bag.

"I stored all of our medications in your refrigerator for the weekend," she said to Norah. Turning to Jim, she commented, "The volunteers were all patient, and they helped the kids gain confidence."

"I wish we could have worked with only one group all summer," Jim continued. "We could gain a better assessment of the program if we'd had the same riders for several months, not weeks."

"Why didn't you?" Norah questioned.

"Since it's a pilot project, our board of directors wanted to see how different groups responded to the therapy. We'll work with the mentally and physically impaired during the next two sessions. That way we can compare our methods and determine what's most effective." He pulled his car keys from his pocket. "We'd better hit the road, Carolyn. We need to stay close behind the vans."

Norah followed them down the walk to their car. "Have the meals been all right? I need to know before I buy groceries tomorrow."

Jim's generous mouth spread into a wide smile. "I didn't hear any complaints, so continue just what you're doing. You're responsible for the cooking—so make your own decisions."

"Next week, I plan to have homemade ice cream. There are a couple of hand-crank freezers here, and the kids might like the experience of making ice cream."

"Sounds like a great idea."

"Also, the Johnsons, Mason and I are planning a special program the last week you're here. We want to take the kids on a short hayride, have a cookout and some music.''

''That's extra work for you, but it sounds like a great idea,'' Jim agreed.

''Then it won't be too dangerous for the children to ride in a wagon?''

''Shouldn't think so,'' Jim said.

After she waved Jim and Carolyn on their way, Norah went to the kitchen where Sheila was filling the dishwasher. They'd made a good team in the kitchen—each of them had agreed on their duties, and they did them without getting in the other's way.

''I feel good about the week,'' Sheila said. ''It seems so rewarding. I like kids, and until Doug and I start on our family, it's kinda fun to be working with these children.''

Norah nodded in agreement. ''They seemed to like our food, and Jim says it's fine.''

''Do you want me to go grocery shopping with you tomorrow?''

''It would be helpful. I need to pick up my car from the mechanic's. Then you could come back home, and I can shop alone. You must have lots of work to do at home.''

''That's true—I haven't cleaned our home all week. I'm so glad one of the volunteers does all the cleaning here.''

"I feel rather mean about being paid for working when these volunteers get nothing," Norah said. "But I really do need the money."

She stood, hands on her hips, looking at several bowls of food on the table. "I don't know what to do with these leftovers. They won't last until Monday. Why don't you telephone Doug and ask him to come and eat supper with us?"

"He and Mason are together," Sheila said. "They went to a machinery sale in Valentine today. They should be on their way home by now. I'll see if Doug will answer his cell phone."

Sheila reached for the phone on the kitchen wall. "Hi," Sheila said, when Doug answered. "Just checking to see where you are." She listened to Doug's answer. "The kids are gone, and we have a lot of food left. We'll wait until you and Mason get here, and you can eat with us."

Replacing the phone, Sheila said, "They'll be home by four o'clock. Doug said all they'd had to eat today was one hamburger and a Coke, so I figure we won't have to worry about leftovers by the time they finish."

Norah tried to conceal her pleasure. She hadn't seen Mason all week, and she looked forward to spending the evening with him. He had telephoned a few times, but they'd both been busy during the daytime, and she went to bed early in the evening.

She figured she looked untidy after spending the day in the kitchen, and she wondered if she'd have time for a shower.

Sheila must have read her thoughts because she said, "I'd like to change into different clothes, but I've fed these two men before, and they'll pay more attention to the food on the table than they will to what we're wearing."

Knowing this was probably true, Norah stopped thinking about her appearance. She mixed the left-over spaghetti and sauce together, added Parmesan cheese and put it in the oven to bake. She set out the gelatin salad left from lunch and filled bowls with raw vegetable salad. She arranged rolls on a plate to pop into the microwave when the men arrived.

"Let's set this small table here in the kitchen rather than eating in the dining room. It seems more homey."

"Good idea! We have plenty of cake and fruit salad left," Sheila said as she cut two large squares of cake for the men and dished up helpings of fruit salad for her and Norah.

"I'll make some coffee," Norah said.

"As hot as the weather has turned," Sheila said, "the guys will probably want iced tea, too, but there's almost a pitcher left."

When the men walked into the kitchen, Doug

grabbed Sheila in a bear hug and kissed her soundly. "I've missed you today, honey."

Norah's face grew warm in embarrassment, and Mason stood awkwardly in the doorway, pulling at his collar. After a few days with Sheila and Doug, Norah had seen how much tenderness and sharing she'd missed by not being married.

She made an effort to regain her composure. "Come in, Mason. Hope you won't mind leftovers."

He hung his hat on a chair by the door. "Not at all." He took her hand. "How's your week been?"

"Rewarding and busy." Her face brightened with animation. "I'm so happy I came here. I felt sorry for the children at first, but by the end of the week, I forgot their disabilities and marveled at their courage. This program is a godsend to them. I hope it can be continued."

"I'm sorry I haven't had time to watch what's going on," Mason said, "but we've been busy at the ranch."

After they'd eaten, Norah and Sheila cleared the table while the men pushed their chairs back, each crossing a leg on his knee, visibly relaxed, and savored an after-dinner cup of coffee. The dude ranch owners had provided many table games for their guests, and Sheila brought a box of Rook cards from the dining room.

"How about a game?" she asked. "We've needed another person so we can play partners in our card games. Norah, do you want to challenge the guys to a game of Rook? When we play single-handed, they always beat me."

"Why not? We can sleep late in the morning."

The time passed quickly as Sheila and Doug pitted their wits against each other. Norah didn't care much who won, and she doubted that Mason did, either, but they joined in the kidding and rivalry between the younger couple. When she and Norah won two games out of three, Sheila crowed, "There! I knew all I needed was a good partner. Another game?"

"No," Doug said, "it's ten o'clock. You and Norah might be able to sleep late in the morning, but I can't. I need to check out all the horses the kids have been riding this week and make necessary repairs to the tack before they come back on Monday. I want to be sure the equipment is safe for the kids. So let's go home."

"I'd better go, too," Mason said after the Johnsons left, but obviously didn't want to leave.

"No need to hurry. I've been under a lot of pressure this week, and I need to relax before bedtime. Shall we sit on the porch?" Norah asked in a quiet voice.

The security light at the barn didn't penetrate this

corner of the house, but Norah turned off most of the lights in the house. Since there was no moon tonight, they more or less groped their way to the chairs on the back porch.

Noting her actions, Mason said, "You must be getting accustomed to country living. You don't seem to fear the darkness now."

"I'm forcing myself to accept it. Most of the time, I'm not afraid at all."

"Are you going to be busy this weekend?" Mason asked.

"Sheila is driving me into Valentine tomorrow so I can pick up my car. I'll buy groceries, and that will about use up the day."

"I'll be busy tomorrow, too. But how about Sunday? If you're not busy, let's go someplace after we attend church service."

"On foot, horseback or vehicle?" she said, and perceiving the lightness of her tone, Mason knew she was smiling.

"Your preference."

"Then let's go in your truck. Aren't there some Mari Sandoz sites in the Sand Hills? I've read her book, *Old Jules,* and I'd like to see the places she mentioned in her writings."

"That's where we'll go then—it's not far away. I've always been interested in that area, too. My great-grandfather came to Nebraska the same time as Old Jules—they were neighbors for a while.''

"Then both of us will find the day interesting.''

"I'll pick you up about nine o'clock on Sunday and we'll go to church in Valentine. It will be a truck this time, but next time, we go on horseback. Have you been riding Daisy?''

"No. I haven't had time.''

"You'll have to make time. Ride in the evening or early morning. It will be relaxing and might make you sleep better.''

"Yes, Doctor!'' she said sarcastically.

"I mean it, Norah. You should learn to ride. I'll come over a few evenings next week and ride with you.''

"All right,'' she said meekly. "But they'll have to be short outings. And speaking of which, we need to start plans for a short wagon trip, campfire and wiener roast at the end of each of these sessions. I noticed several wagons in the sheds, so if the children are still uneasy about going on horseback, they can ride in a wagon.''

"That's a great idea. Doug and I will arrange it, if the H & H staff approve.''

"Jim Hanson has already okayed it.''

"And the four of us will entertain the kids with some music?''

"I don't know how entertaining it will be, but I told Jim we'd sing."

"I'd better go," Mason said, standing very close to Norah. He fidgeted from one foot to the other, more ill at ease than he could remember. What was there about this woman that caused him to act like he was fifteen again? He hadn't had a peaceful night's sleep since Norah had come into his life. He wasn't used to having his emotions in such a turmoil. He was middle-aged, for goodness' sake, too late for him to contemplate romance in his life.

But his heart didn't seem to agree with his thoughts. As his shoulder touched hers, Mason longed to kiss her, but he listened to his head instead of his heart. Instead of kissing her, he patted her on the shoulder and hurried off the porch before he did something foolish.

"Goodbye. Until Sunday," Norah called after him.

Mason usually telephoned almost every day, but since she would see him the next day, Norah was surprised to receive his call on Saturday night. "We'll be doing some walking in the Sandoz country, so you might want to wear jeans and comfortable shoes."

"Thanks for letting me know, Mason. I'd been wondering."

"We'll eat lunch in Valentine, but the rest of the time we'll be in the wide-open spaces. You'll see cowboy country at its best. It's a hundred miles from Valentine to Gordon, which is in the heart of Old Jules country. We'll be late getting home."

"The children don't arrive until noon on Mondays, so I'll have plenty of time to be ready for them, but I'll prepare some things in advance tomorrow before we go."

Leaving Valentine on Sunday after lunch for the drive to Gordon, mile after mile they traveled without seeing another vehicle or any sign of life, except for herds of cattle gathered around windmills. After they traveled for a long time in silence, Mason said, "Penny for your thoughts."

"This scenery is beautiful," Norah said, "but it seems so desolate. It's fine, driving along in this comfortable truck, but I can't help think how intimidating this land would have been to the pioneers."

She laughed lightly, but Mason noticed that her hands were clenched tightly in her lap. No doubt she was thinking about how dark it would have been.

"Especially for the women!" Norah continued, staring straight ahead at the undulating grassland that stretched into infinity. "No doubt the man would have had the vision to take up new land, and the wife would have followed his lead. There wouldn't have been any telephones, no doctors, no neighbors, no churches. I don't believe I'd have made a good pioneer.''

Although Mason normally gloried in the beauty of this area, for some reason, Norah's words depressed him. ''It was a hard life, and many settlers couldn't stand it. They soon gave up their claims and moved back to civilization. I guess that's the reason I'm proud of my ancestors. They wanted land of their own and they suffered to get it.'' He paused, his thoughts turning to the fact that he had no progeny to take the land his ancestors had struggled to settle. As he had many times before, Mason wished he'd remarried.

During the afternoon, as they toured the area where Mari Sandoz had lived as a child, and had immortalized the neighborhood in the biography of her father, *Old Jules,* Norah seemed to throw off the melancholy that had affected her as they'd traveled.

The Sandoz places had few visitors, so Mason and Norah were able to enjoy the museum that was a replica of Mari's studio in Greenwich Village. They walked to her grave, and again Norah thought of the isolation, wondering why the noted author chose such a lonely burial site.

To return home after leaving the Sandoz memorials, Mason turned eastward on Route 2 and traveled to the town of Thedford. From there, he accessed the Flying K ranch on Route 83.

Norah had a deep desire to fit into Mason's world, and she was uncomfortable that the open prairie still intimidated her. She was eager to have many of her doubts about the future erased, but after a month in Mason's company, her doubts had compounded instead of eased. When her work at the Bar 8 was finished and she left the Sand Hills, she wanted to feel good about all of her summer's experiences. The work with H & H was rewarding, and although cooking three meals a day wasn't the missionary work she'd envisioned, still she was "doing unto the least of these," as Jesus had instructed His disciples. She believed her work at the Bar 8 fulfilled that command of Jesus.

She didn't doubt that she was doing God's will, but when she started to be satisfied with her life as it was, her thoughts turned to Mason. He was the hidden factor in her future. When God had directed her steps toward the Sand Hills, had Mason been a part of His plan for her? Or was he just a casual acquaintance to leave behind at summer's end?

Chapter Nine

Mason placed his hand on her shoulder, and Norah roused out of reverie, realizing that they'd turned off the highway toward the ranches. "Thanks, Mason. It's been a nice day."

"You've been so quiet the past several miles, I wasn't sure you enjoyed yourself."

"Sorry I haven't been better company, but I'm not a very talkative person. I spend a lot of time alone with my thoughts."

"I can understand that," he said. "Sometimes I think I spend too much time thinking myself."

For the past two weeks, he'd believed that Norah could become a permanent fixture in his life. But today he'd fretted because Norah seemed frightened of the environment. He'd assumed that she'd mastered her fear of the darkness, but now she seemed disturbed by the isolation of the area. On the other hand, Mason couldn't understand how anyone could exist in a city with people living all around them. Could country and city ever mix?

"Sheila told me that even now there are long periods of time in the winter when you can't leave the ranch."

"Sometimes we have blizzards that close the highways. But I never mind that—it's a good opportunity to do work on the buildings."

"And just think of all the knitting and quilting a person could accomplish during times like that," Norah said lightly, so Mason decided she must not be as disturbed as he'd thought.

"You enjoy your needlework?"

"Yes. I had lots of time on my hands when I was taking care of my family, and I'm not one to sit with idle hands. I make items for mission hospitals and long-term care facilities in Missouri, as well as for my family and friends. I enjoy creating pretty things, and it's good therapy for my hands and mind."

Dusk was falling when they arrived at the Bar 8, so Mason walked to the door with Norah and checked the downstairs to be sure all was safe. When he stepped out on the porch, Mason turned and came back to where Norah stood at the foot of the stairs. Without a word, he placed his hands on her shoulders, bent and kissed her cheek. He pushed stray tendrils back from her face before he turned toward the door.

What an unpredictable man! Norah thought as he drove away. But unpredictable in a nice way. Even after she went to bed, Norah could still feel the warm touch of his lips.

Norah marveled at the change three weeks had made in the H & H riders. She spent some of her free time observing the work in the arena or on the outdoor trail course. The volunteers with more horse experience served as mount leaders, while others walked beside the riders to give physical support as needed, to ensure the safety of the children and to reinforce the instruction of the therapist.

Discussing the matter with Sheila, Norah said, "I'd like to do more than just cook for the riders, but I don't want to leave you with extra work. If you're interested in volunteering, we can coordinate our schedules."

"I've been wondering how I could manage to help. I rode a horse long before I could drive a truck, but the H & H directors are very particular about how their horses are handled. But surely there's some way my horse sense can be put to use. Let's talk to Jim and see what we can do. I know they can use more help."

Jim was enthusiastic about the prospect of more volunteers. "Oh, yes, I can use you! You can start out with grooming and tack, then practice with the trained mount leaders and sidewalkers."

Sheila and Norah arranged to volunteer at least an hour with H & H each day, and the volunteer work left a deep impression on Norah. As she watched the blind children learning to trust their horses, she learned a lot to improve her own riding skills. The young riders seemed to gain confidence when she related that she'd only recently started learning how to ride a horse. She was gratified that she had learned a basic knowledge of riding from Mason, but as she helped the children, she continued to learn.

The wagon ride and campfire was planned for the Thursday night before the first group of children finished their course.

"This would be a good time to celebrate their accomplishments," Jim Hanson said. "Carolyn and I will come up with some awards, so each one can take home a certificate. We'll present those around the campfire."

"We can picnic in a grove of oak trees just around the bend in the river," Sheila said. "It's not more than two miles—and a level, easy trail."

"That will be perfect," Jim said. "I think we should transport everyone by wagon. Some of the children aren't up to riding that far yet, and it would be better to have all of them feel equal.''

''Doug and I will drive two wagons filled with plenty of hay,'' Mason said when they discussed the plan with him.

''Sheila and I will go earlier than the rest of you and take the food by truck,'' Norah said.

''No fair,'' Doug joked. ''I don't think you want to ride on the wagon. We're trying to make you into a country woman.''

''I've already had enough countrifying to last out the summer,'' Norah assured him.

The Niobrara, a shallow stream with occasional sandbars, was wide at the curve in the river. The wind had been strong all day, but in the cove, only a slight breeze riffled the cottonwood leaves. Doug had gone earlier in the day to mow the grass at the picnic area and to arrange the wood for the fire. He'd also cut twigs from the willow bushes for the kids to use in roasting hot dogs and marshmallows.

Sheila and Norah set up several folding tables and chairs to provide seating. Sheila volunteered to tend the fire when Norah meekly admitted she'd never started a campfire.

''We all have our talents,'' Sheila assured her. ''I sure can't make cookies like these,'' she added as she picked up a large no-bake cookie from a tray that Norah was arranging on the table.

They'd prepared the condiments for the hot dogs, cheese cubes and a plate of raw vegetables earlier in the day. Sheila set out the mustard, ketchup and chopped onions while she took another peanut-butter cookie from the tray.

"Promise to teach me how to cook, and I'll teach you to make a campfire," she said to Norah.

"Deal!" Norah agreed.

"Doug will be glad to have you give me cooking lessons. I've always been a tomboy and loved to be outside helping Dad, so I'm just learning to cook. We've only been married a year."

The sound of singing preceded the wagons before they came in sight. Even the children who were to-tally blind exhibited happy faces as they rode into the cove. The Seeing Eye dogs hovered close as their charges climbed off the wagons.

The children were all city kids who'd never been on a hayride, nor had they participated in a wiener roast. Jim Hanson gave Norah a thumbs-up when the kids gathered around the fire, extending sticks that held more than one hot dog. The volunteers encouraged the children to do as much of the roast-ing as they could.

Mason stood to one side watching Norah as she efficiently served the children and anticipated their every need. She was compassionate to the children, but **not** to the point that she discouraged them from exercising their independence.

He was convinced she could have been a wonderful wife and mother, and he wondered if she had any interest in a midlife marriage.

Norah's eyes intercepted his glance across the campfire, and he felt his face flushing. He hoped she couldn't read his thoughts.

Doug, who stood beside Mason, nudged him in the side and said out of the corner of his mouth, ''Want me to give you some advice on how to win the fair lady?''

''No, thank you.''

''It'll be a mistake if you let her get away from you. Sheila thinks Norah likes you.''

''When did the two of you become matchmakers?''

''When you started making sheep eyes at Norah.''

Mason didn't answer, and Doug insisted, ''I'm serious, Mason. You could have had your pick of any single girl in this community for the past twenty years, but none of them stirred you up like Norah has. You should give her some serious thought.''

As if I haven't been thinking about her constantly, Mason thought, but he was spared an answer when Sheila brought two filled plates to them. ''Norah's promised to teach me to cook, Doug. Does that make you happy?''

''I'm already happy.''

Sheila's face brightened, and she stood on tiptoe to kiss Doug on the lips. Mason was used to their public display of devotion, and usually he wasn't envious, but tonight he seemed to realize what he'd missed by living alone. His eyes strayed to Norah again. Was Doug right? Did she like him, too?

The coals had burned to embers when Doug swung the guitar over his shoulder.

''C'mon, kids,'' he said. ''Let's sing.''

He led them in several Bible choruses, then he tipped his hat back on his forehead, saying in a joking voice, ''Now you're in for a *real* treat. Tonight marks the first appearance of a new Western singing group—Johnson, King and Williamson, soon to be known as the Flying K Wranglers. Just remember someday, when these names appear in the bright lights of Branson or Nashville, that you heard the premiere performance.''

They sung some of the old favorites, ''Sweet Betsy from Pike,'' and ''Home on the Range,'' closing with a hymn, ''Now the Day is Over.'' Norah wasn't so confident of her singing talent, but the other three had good voices.

Norah and Sheila stayed on after the wagons left to be sure the fire was extinguished, and using the headlights of the truck, they picked up any stray trash that might have escaped.

Sheila yawned noticeably as they drove toward the ranch buildings. "Gee, I'm tired," she said. "And we have to be up early to prepare a good breakfast for this group's farewell meal."

"But we'll have a whole week to recover."

"Ha!" Sheila jeered. "Have you forgotten that next Thursday is the Fourth of July celebration at the Flying K? That will take a lot of work."

"And I don't have a costume to wear. I intended to order one, but it's too late now."

"I have several outfits I've used in other years. You can wear one of those."

"Hardly! I weigh about twenty pounds more than you do, and I'm a few inches shorter."

"I have a pioneer woman's dress that you can hem, and it has a full skirt. It will probably work, or you can borrow a dress from my mother—she's about your build. She tells me that she was my size when she was a girl, but she gained weight when she had her babies, and never lost it."

Laughing, Norah said, "I don't even have that excuse!" Weight had become a touchy subject with Norah this summer, so she asked, "What kind of a costume are you wearing this year?"

"I'm going as Calamity Jane."

"Who?"

"Calamity Jane—probably the Wild West's most notorious woman. Legend has it that she was an orphan raised by soldiers at Fort Laramie. She became famous as a stage driver and a bullwhacker—that's an ox-team driver."

"Will it be difficult to portray her?"

"Nah," Sheila said. "I'll wear a pair of Doug's dirty jeans, a coat—three sizes too big for me that I borrowed from my father-in-law—and one of his worn-out slouch hats. I'll not indulge in Calamity's tobacco chewing and swearing."

"Seems like you could have found a better role model to portray," Norah commented humorously.

"Oh, Calamity had her good points. In her heyday, she was a pretty woman, and when Deadwood, South Dakota, was ravaged with a smallpox epidemic, she was the best nurse in town. Legend holds that she got 'religion' in her later years."

"Just goes to show you can't judge a book by its cover, as the old saying goes."

When they drove into the ranch yard right behind the wagons, Mason called, "Leave those tables and chairs in the truck. We'll unload them as soon as we stable the horses."

While Doug and Mason stored the equipment and supplies in the proper places, Sheila and Norah made preliminary plans for breakfast. Sheila put the place settings on the table. Norah mixed a batch of bran muffin batter to stand in the refrigerator overnight and prepared fresh fruit to marinate in apple cider.

When the men finished their work, Norah said, "You go on home, Sheila. All I have to do it cut up this leftover ham to put in the scrambled eggs. It won't take long for us to finish the meal in the morning."

Mason perched on a stool and leaned on the working island in the middle of the kitchen. He watched Norah in silence as she moved around the room. His watchful eyes made her somewhat uncomfortable.

To break the silence, she said, "Do you think the campfire idea is a good way to end the group's activities?"

"I thought so. And Jim was enthusiastic about it. He asked us to have a campfire on the closing night for the other two groups, too. How'd it work from your angle?"

"No problem at all. We used disposable plates and cups, so the work was easier. It's been a rewarding three weeks."

"I haven't been as closely involved as you've been, but it's apparently been successful. Even I can notice a difference in the kids from the first week."

"If the other two sessions go as well as this one, H & H will probably be able to continue."

"That's what Jim said. He wanted to know if the ranch would be available next year."

Norah's heart fluttered a little at that information. Already she was dreading the end of the summer when she'd be finished at the Bar 8. Or was it Mason she didn't want to leave? If she did enroll in college, and the program continued next year, perhaps she could spend another summer in the Sand Hills. A few months away from Mason would give her a better perspective on her feelings for him.

"What did you tell Jim?"

"Nothing. I've got a lot of money invested in the Bar 8, and I can't continue to operate it at a loss as I've been doing. The amount H & H is paying for the summer is a pittance. I wish I was rich enough to let them use the property without cost, but I'm not. Most ranchers are land poor—lots of land, but not much money. So if I have an offer for the Bar 8 this winter, I'll have to take it."

So much for her plans for another summer, Norah thought as she sat opposite Mason.

"The summer is moving too fast for me," Mason said and he reached across the table and lifted Norah's hand. "You've been here almost six weeks, and it's going to be time for you to leave before I'm ready for it. When you came, you were looking for answers of where to go from here. Have you reached any conclusions?"

Her fingers curled around his. "No, not really. I suppose I keep hoping that the summer will never end."

"Then you do like it here."

"Very much so. I like the work, and also the country, once I got used to the solitude." Her eyelids fluttered downward. "And I like the people, too. You've been very kind to me, Mason."

"That hasn't been hard to do. You're special to me, Norah. You've given a lift to my spirits that I haven't felt for years."

He released her hand and walked around the table. "Ever since you've been here, I've wanted to kiss you. Would you mind very much if I kissed you now?"

Her eyes were still downcast, and she felt a flush spread over her face. She decided she shouldn't admit how often she wondered what it would be like to have his kiss. *This is your opportunity, Norah, don't muff it,* her thoughts prodded.

She lifted her head. "No, Mason, I wouldn't mind at all."

Eagerly, he pulled her upward and squeezed her so hard that Norah gasped. Not since her teenage years had she been held in a man's arms, and she was nervous about it. But something in Mason's manner soothed her as he eased his grasp and held her as if she were a priceless item that he cherished.

At first, his heavy whiskers brushing against her face startled her. Then she felt a ripple of excitement as the slow caress of his lips on her cheek and mouth awakened emotions that had lain buried for years. The kiss seemed to envelop her, but she was sorry when he slowly lifted his head and stepped back.

Mason's lips moved as if he wanted to say something, but couldn't find the words. He leaned over her again and placed a soft kiss on her lips.

''Thank you, Norah, and good night.''

The room felt empty when Mason stepped outside and closed the door. Norah held a fist to her lips, wondering how much Mason's embrace would affect her plans for the future. Would any place she traveled to, at home or abroad, feel empty if Mason wasn't there?

Chapter Ten

On Monday morning, Sheila, Doug and Norah gathered at the Flying K ranch to help prepare for the July Fourth celebration. Norah and Sheila tackled the house—cleaned the windows, washed the curtains, scrubbed the floors, polished the woodwork and furniture.

"I clean the house for Mason every few weeks," Sheila said, "but I only do a major cleaning once a year. It's nice to have some help doing it today."

"The house is rather small and shouldn't take a long time. And it's a pleasure to work here. It's such a homey place. The first time I saw the house, it seemed to welcome me."

"A lot of living has taken place within these walls. The two bedrooms and bathroom are in the original house where Mason's grandparents lived. His dad modernized the place, and added this large all-purpose room before he died. It's a comfortable home, and being a one-floor layout, it's easy to keep warm and cozy in the winter.''

"The house at the Bar 8 is probably hard to heat.''

"Yes, it is. That's one reason Mason wants to sell the place. The upkeep is expensive. When we moved to the Bar 8, we chose to take the small house because our utilities cost much less there.''

"I like the house though,'' Norah said. "It reminds me of my home in Missouri, which I'm also selling because I can't afford the upkeep.''

"If you sell it, maybe you can buy the Bar 8.''

"I'd be jumping out of the frying pan into the fire. If Mason can't afford the place, I surely can't. I must find a job of some kind as soon as the summer is over.''

"We like having you for a neighbor,'' Sheila said with a sly glance in Norah's direction. "You and Mason might go into partnership on the Bar 8.''

Norah gave strict attention to the chair she was polishing. What kind of partnership was Sheila suggesting? Did she suspect the spark that flared between Norah and Mason each time they met? Norah wouldn't look at Sheila, fearful her face would betray the secret of her heart.

Hearing a mower move by the window, Norah said, "Sounds like Doug is getting the grass mown."

"Yes, he's doing that while Mason digs the pit for the ox-roast. Ever tasted pit-roasted beef?"

"No."

"It's delicious. Why don't you take a break and go watch what Mason's doing? It's an interesting process, and he'd probably welcome a glass of lemonade about now."

"It would be a relief to be out in the fresh air. This scented furniture polish is a bit overpowering."

Following the sound of the tractor, Norah found Mason behind the machinery shed, using a front-end loader to dig the pit. He waved to her, and she held up the glass of lemonade. He smiled and nodded his head. She watched as he finished the pit that looked about eight feet long and half as wide. When he stopped the tractor, Norah peered down into the pit that was over five feet deep.

"Thought you might be thirsty."

Wiping his forehead with a bandana, he said, "Thirsty and hot! Come sit here in the shade of the barn." They leaned their backs against the silo, and he took the glass and downed half of the liquid in one long swallow.

"Looks like I should have brought the whole pitcher. How much more do you have to do?"

"That's all the digging with the front-end loader, but I'll use a shovel and make the sides straight, so the dirt won't crumble after we start the fire."

"Sounds like a lot of work, but Sheila says the finished product is worth it."

"You're right on both counts. About two days before the ox-roast, I'll pile some wood into the pit, start burning it and keep adding fuel until there's a thick bed of coals. About midnight the day before the picnic, we'll put the meat on the coals."

"How much beef?"

"I took a steer to the butcher, and I don't know how much it weighed, but he'll cut the best part of the beef into six-pound pieces, and we'll roast enough to feed about a hundred people. Doug's mother will bake two roasts in a conventional oven, shred the meat and barbeque it. The rest we'll slice and serve on buns or just on the plate. The butcher will make the rest into hamburger, or smaller roasts, and I'll have lots of meat for the freezer."

"I'm looking forward to tasting it. Thinking about the feast that's coming, the potato soup I prepared for lunch doesn't sound very appetizing."

"If you made it, I'll like it," Mason assured her. "I'm ready to eat."

They moved back into the house and settled down to lunch. While they ate a leisurely lunch, Sheila said, "Norah, we'll have to figure out a costume for you. Mom said you're welcome to wear some of the outfits she has. She and Dad are coming for supper tonight, and she'll bring several dresses.''

"Don't spend a lot of time finding something for me to wear. Surely some people come in ordinary clothes? Everyone will know I'm a visitor."

"It's more fun if you're in costume," Sheila insisted.

The next morning, Sheila came to the Bar 8 ranch house with several plastic garment bags.

"Here you are," she said. "Take your pick."

The choice lay between a Sioux maiden's buckskin outfit, the gaudy dress of a dance hall girl and a calico prairie dress with a matching bonnet.

"The choice isn't hard," Norah said, laughing. "I don't have the features to portray a Sioux woman, and I can imagine how I'd look in that dance hall dress. I'll be more comfortable in the prairie woman's outfit."

"I figured that would be your choice," Sheila said, "but Mom insisted I bring all of them. By the way," she added, "we need some more songs for the party. Mason is coming tonight so we can practice."

Wednesday evening, Norah went with Doug and Sheila to the Flying K to help prepare the meat for roasting. The butcher had wrapped fifteen roasts in two thicknesses of butcher's paper, to which they added two thicknesses of aluminum foil, and wrapped it all in four layers of newspapers.

After that, the packets were bound with stainless-steel wire, dipped into a tub of water and quickly laid on top of the hot coals about a foot below ground level. Doug placed a flat piece of steel on the packages, and he and Mason quickly shoveled eighteen inches of dirt on top of the steel plate.

It was quite late when all the preparations were finished and the Johnsons and Norah left the Flying K.

"There'll be a lot of vehicles at the party," Sheila volunteered when they dropped Norah off at the Bar 8 ranch house. "If you like, we'll stop by and get you in the morning."

"Fine."

Norah both anticipated and dreaded meeting Mason's neighbors. Because of the quiet life she'd lived, it was hard for Norah to move out of her comfort zone. She was at ease with the few people she'd met since she'd arrived in Nebraska, but she was a little anxious about being introduced to seventy or more people. The Sand Hills seemed deserted when you drove along the highway, but many ranch headquarters were located several miles off the main roads. Obviously, the neighbors didn't socialize much, so anyone who lived in this area would have to become accustomed to solitude. Could she?

They arrived at the ranch at seven o'clock to make last-minute preparations. Mason put his hands on Norah's shoulders and held her off to take a good look at her blue calico dress and sunbonnet. "You look as pretty as a picture," he said, heedless of the amused glances of Sheila and Doug.

Norah blushed a little at his compliment, but she said, "Thank you. But I don't feel like myself. I'd rather have spent the day in shorts or pants, but I bowed to custom."

Mason didn't look any different than usual, because the ranchers still dressed much like they had in pioneer days. Admittedly, Mason's name-brand jeans and hand-tooled boots were more expensive than his ancestors might have worn, but otherwise, his attire could easily have been used a century earlier.

Doug's parents came before the other guests, and Norah enjoyed meeting this couple who had known Mason all of his life.

Clapping Paul Johnson fondly on the back, Mason said to Norah, "This man knows everything there is to know about me, but I hope he doesn't tell all he knows."

"Yeah," Paul said, his eyes crinkling in his

weathered skin. "We played hooky from school more than once, and we stood up with each other at our weddings. We've been through a lot together. I could tell you lots of things, and most of them are good."

Norah felt a little self-conscious standing beside Mason in the ranch yard, shaking hands with, and greeting, the guests, almost as if she were Mason's wife. Did she detect a measure of pride in Mason's voice as he introduced her to his neighbors?

What would her life be like if she could stand by this man's side until death parted them? Did she really love Mason? She hoped not, for her heart still beckoned toward an overseas mission ministry. But at other times, she wished she could give her full-time devotion to Mason. Norah had a divided heart, and it was making her miserable.

Although Mason tried to hide the fact, he was so proud to have Norah beside him, he could have pitched his hat into the air and shouted a jubilee. Since his father's death, he'd stood alone to greet his neighbors. He suddenly remembered the scene in the Garden of Eden when God had provided a mate for Adam. God said, "It is not good that man should be alone."

Of course, Eve had always been blamed for bringing a lot of trouble to Adam, but the pleasure of having Norah beside him convinced Mason that Eve had brought Adam more happiness than trouble. If God said that man shouldn't live alone, Mason King had wasted a lot of years.

By midmorning, the fields surrounding the ranch house were crowded with vehicles, and neighbors excitedly visited on this rare occasion when they could all get together.

The first event of the day was judging the whisker-growing contest, and when Norah saw some of the other ranchers, she knew Mason didn't have a chance of winning. He didn't even place among the top ten contestants, whose whiskers looked like brush piles.

Mason's hands threaded the heavy beard on his own face, and whispered to Norah, "Never again! I can't wait until tomorrow when I'll gladly take up shaving again."

Sheila came in second place with her Calamity Jane outfit, and shouted with laughter when her prize was a piggy bank that squealed when you tried to remove any money.

"I wish I'd known there was such a gadget," Doug shouted. "I'd have bought one for her when we got married."

The guests had brought lawn chairs, and after the judging, and awarding of trophies, they gathered around two well-laden hay wagons that Mason had placed beside two large cottonwood trees in the pasture, trees that his grandmother had planted.

After lunch, there were horse races for all ages, and Norah was amazed at the skill of very young children. There was even a greenhorn race, which Doug tried to persuade Norah to enter, but she absolutely refused. She'd embarrass herself as well as Mason if she exhibited her poor horsemanship before his neighbors.

The guests stayed through the supper hour, still enjoying the succulent roast beef and other foods left over from the noon meal. The fireworks were to be the last event of the day. But before darkness fell, the newly formed quartet presented their special music, which was well received by the audience.

The fireworks, ably administered by a firm from Omaha, spread a vivid display of lights across the prairie sky, bringing the day to a spectacular close. When the last sparkling burst of light flashed across the heavens, the ranchers headed for home, for although it was the start of the July Fourth weekend, for ranchers it was a workday like any other.

When no one was left except for Doug and Sheila, Norah and Mason, Sheila sat down on the porch floor with a sigh.

''Boy, am I glad that's over for another year!''

''You can be a guest next year, and that doesn't take so much work,'' Norah said.

"No such luck. My parents will be hosting next year."

"But you love it," Doug said.

"Sure do! Well, let's go home," Sheila said. "Ready, Norah?"

Mason cleared his throat. "You might as well stay a while, Norah. I'll take you to the Bar 8 later on this evening."

"Well, it can't get much later than this," Doug said, looking at his watch. "It's almost midnight."

Mason didn't reply to Doug's good-natured wise-crack, so he and Sheila climbed into their truck and whirled out of the driveway.

"Hope you didn't mind staying," Mason said as they sat together on the cushioned glider. "It takes a while for me to unwind after such a shindig, and I wanted company. Did you enjoy yourself?"

"Yes, I did. It was a totally new experience for me. You have wonderful neighbors."

"Is it a place you could settle down and live?" Mason asked, not looking at her. "You're at loose ends now, so you might want to relocate to the Sand Hills."

His comment startled Norah. Mason knew she needed to work to make a living. He also knew she wanted to go to college and ultimately to the mission field. What was he implying? If Norah had an answer to that question, she might also be able to find answers to many other things that plagued her.

Could she have mistaken God's call? If God had wanted her to be a missionary, wouldn't He have made the way easy for her? She'd lived a life of service for her family. Would God put His approval on a new life with Mason? It was a difficult question.

"Don't answer if you'd rather not," Mason prompted.

"I like the people, and I'm getting used to the solitude, but I have many things to sort out in my mind and heart."

"Norah, have you been in contact with your family since you've been here?"

She was silent for a moment, but she shook her head. "No. I didn't leave a forwarding address. The Realtor who's listing my house is a friend of the family, and he knows where I am. I telephoned him and gave him the telephone number at the Bar 8 so he could contact me. If my family wants to get in touch with me, they can find out where I am. I'm not sure they want any further contact with me, and I won't push myself on them."

"The Bible says that the person who's been wronged should take the first step toward reconciliation."

"I know that, and I may do it someday, but why

not let me enjoy the summer without having to deal with that situation?''

"I'm sorry, Norah. I shouldn't have meddled—it's just that all of my life I've wished I had brothers and sisters. So it bothers me that you're estranged from yours, and I think it bothers you, too.''

"Very much so,'' Norah agreed, "but I'm not ready to deal with it yet. I told you before, that when I look closely at myself, I don't particularly like what I see.''

Mason put his arm around her shoulders in a brotherly gesture. "On the other hand, when I look at you, I *like* what I see.''

She darted a quick glance in his direction as he continued. "Surely my opinion doesn't surprise you. I wanted to tell you when you said that before, but I thought it was inappropriate to say that on such short acquaintance.''

"Thanks,'' Norah said. "I probably will have to make the first overture to heal the breach between us, but the time isn't right yet.''

"Forgive me for meddling?'' he asked.

"Of course. I know what I have to do, but I can't do it yet.''

With shoulders touching, they moved in rhythm as the glider slowly moved back and forth. Norah was sensitive to the sound of insects, and the bark of a coyote in the distance that caused her to shiver. Mason's arm tightened, and he drew Norah closer with his head leaning against hers. It was a time of tranquillity and silence, rather than for speaking, and they talked no more of the matters nearest to their hearts.

Chapter Eleven

Since it had been two o'clock before Mason had brought her back to the Bar 8, Norah hadn't expected to see him at all the next day. But she was working in the kitchen about noon when she heard his firm tread coming across the dining room floor. When she turned to greet him, she shrieked, "Mason!"

He'd shaved! The lower half of his face was as pearly-white as a baby's skin, while the upper half was tanned to a leathery brown. His lips were sensitive, yet firm, and his face, broad at the eye level, narrowed to a square jaw. His profile was strong and rigid. His hair, now short and manageable, still showed tinges of gray at the temples. Norah moved close to him and ran a hand over his smooth face.

"Why, Mason, you're a handsome man!"

"I was standing in front of the barbershop in Valentine when the barber arrived this morning. It took over an hour for him to get all that brush off of my face. No more whisker-growing contests for me." He put his arm around her. "I have lots of work to do, but I wanted to show you the results."

"I'm glad you did. I've often wondered what you *really* looked like. Want some lunch before you go back to work?"

"No, thanks, I ate a big meal before I left Valentine." He stepped back into the dining room and returned with a long florist's box, which he handed to Norah.

"Here's a thank-you gift for filling in as my hostess yesterday. I really appreciated it."

Her blue eyes widened with astonishment, and words seemed to lodge in her throat. She took the box silently, opened it with trembling hands, gasping at the fragrant scent and the beauty of a dozen pink rosebuds. She swallowed hard, stifled a sob and lifted one of the long-stemmed roses to her face.

"They're beautiful," she said at last. "I don't know what to say." She lifted his hand and kissed it.

Seeing her reaction, Mason also had trouble retaining his composure. He hadn't shed a tear since his father's death, but now his throat constricted and, embarrassed, he swiped at his eyes.

Clearing his throat, he said, "It's the least I could do for the way you helped out."

"It's not a little thing," she said. "I've lived forty-two years, and this is the first time I've ever been given a bouquet of roses."

Trying to lighten the tension, Mason said, "I can top that—I've lived forty-five years, and this is the first time I've ever bought anyone a dozen roses."

Norah placed the box on the table, and laughing gently, she put her arms around Mason's waist, burying her face against his broad chest. His hands drew her closer and she enjoyed the feel of his arms around her. She lifted her face and their lips met in a lingering kiss, amazing Norah at the difference now that he was smooth-shaven.

When she reluctantly withdrew from his embrace, Mason said huskily, "I'd have given you roses long ago if I'd known you'd respond this way."

He touched her earlobe with his lips, whispering in her ear, "I'll be gone for a few days on a business trip to the eastern part of the state. I'll miss you, Norah."

"I'll miss you, too, but I'll be here when you come home."

Norah hadn't gotten well acquainted with any of the volunteers who'd come the first four weeks, but by the time the second group of children came, she and Sheila had their work organized so they both could spend a few hours each day volunteering for the H & H activities.

The second group of children, this time with physical handicaps, required more help in mounting than the first group had needed. Most of the time, Norah used her meager knowledge to help with the tacking up and untacking after each session, but occasionally, she trained as a sidewalker with an experienced volunteer.

She was often thrown into the company of Louis Masters, who'd approached her one day for information about fastening the cinch on a saddle.

Finding this amusing, Norah said, "You're asking a poor teacher," and explained that until six weeks ago, she'd never ridden a horse. "But I've learned enough to saddle my own horse."

"Then that's more than I can do," he said in a well-modulated, kind voice. "I'm an amateur at this, and still training with the more experienced workers."

She helped him finish saddling the horse, and as he led the animal away to the arena, he said, "I notice you sit on the porch in the evening. Do you mind if I come to talk to you after we've finished our work?"

Norah hesitated. Mason was due back from his business trip soon, and since evenings were the only time they could be together, she kept those times for him. But she couldn't see any other reason to refuse.

"I get up at five o'clock, so I can't stay up late, but you're welcome to come sometimes. It won't take me long to tell you everything I know. Mason King, the man who owns this ranch, is the one to give you pointers on handling horses."

"I didn't intend to talk about the H & H program. I just thought I'd enjoy your company. Being quite a lot older than most of the volunteers, I don't have much in common with them. I suppose I'm a bit lonely."

This comment flustered Norah, and she stammered, "Oh! I—I guess that will be all right. When you see me on the porch, you'll know I've finished my work for the day."

Louis Masters turned out to be an interesting conversationalist. A mild-mannered man of medium height, with dark hair and gray eyes framed with dark-rimmed glasses, Louis appeared to be in his late fifties. Norah soon realized that he possessed a great compassion for the children he was helping. And he really caught Norah's attention when he told her that he was a missionary.

"At the present, I'm on furlough from my mis-

sion station in Africa,'' he said, ''and I'll be returning there at the end of the summer.''

''What's the focus of your missionary work?''
Norah inquired.

''I have a Master of Divinity degree, and cur-
rently I'm assigned to a seminary in the Congo,
training native pastors to carry on their work. Modern missionaries don't take leadership roles, as was
the custom in the early days of overseas missions.
We're there to help and encourage the local leaders
in their work. My wife and I have worked in Africa
for ten years.''

For some reason, Norah was relieved to find out
that Louis was married, until he continued, ''My
wife became sick with a terminal disease, and six
months ago, I brought her back to the States to die.
She passed on four months ago, so at the end of the
summer, I'll be returning to Africa alone.''

Norah expressed her sympathy to Louis, and after
he excused himself and left, Norah rocked back and
forth slowly, thoughtful and troubled, until darkness
blanketed the ranch. Why hadn't she told Louis she
wanted to be a missionary? Right from the beginning, she'd believed God had brought her to the Bar
8 for a purpose. During the past few weeks, she'd
started hoping that the reason was twofold—to show
her that working with the clients of H & H was

missionary work, and to find a place in her life for Mason.

Had she completely misjudged God's purpose? If she mentioned to Louis that she was interested in the mission field, would he misunderstand her motive? But she must talk to him about her interest in overseas missions. He was the logical person to advise her about training for the work she believed God wanted her to do.

When Louis came the next night, Norah told him about her call to mission work and how it was delayed because of her family's misfortunes.

"With your experience, perhaps you can advise me. I have only a high school education. How much college would I need to qualify for overseas missions? Or is it too late for me to receive a missionary appointment?"

"That will depend on the denomination you approach about serving. Some denominational standards might exclude your appointment, but if God wants you on the mission field, there'll be a way provided for you to serve."

"I believe that, too, but God hasn't laid that way out for me."

"Some steps we have to take on faith. All of us would like to see what's around the next bend, but it isn't always revealed to us. God expects us to trust Him for the unknown."

"I'm praying that by the end of the summer, I'll have a clear vision of which way to go. But even if I don't have complete assurance, perhaps I'll have enough knowledge to make the right decision."

"I'll join you in praying for direction. I'm sure you have a great contribution to make to overseas missions. And even if you can't receive a full-time appointment, every field is in constant need of short-term volunteers, who come at their own expense and stay six months or more to work on a single project."

Norah didn't have the financial resources to serve without pay, but she would have it if she sold the house in Springfield. Being a part-time missionary was better than not serving at all. Louis's assurance that she could find a place in God's overseas mission outreach should have brought a song to Norah's heart, but, for some reason, her heart didn't feel like singing.

A week passed before Mason returned from his business trip. He stopped at the Flying K only long enough to unload the wagons he'd bought in Omaha before he rushed to the Bar 8. He'd never dreamed he could miss anyone as much as he had Norah. It felt as if he'd left part of himself behind when he'd told her goodbye.

His eagerness to see her suffered a setback when

he parked his pickup in front of the ranch house. Norah sat on the porch, and she had company—a well-groomed, handsome stranger sitting in the rocking chair that Mason usually sat in. The presence of the man upset him.

Norah's slight blush when she introduced Louis made Mason even more uneasy.

Perhaps Louis sensed the tension between Norah and Mason, for he excused himself soon after Mason's arrival and returned to his dormitory room. Mason wanted to demand to know why she was talking to the man, but he knew that reaction would be downright childish. He had no right to monitor Norah's friendships.

"Seems like a nice fellow," Mason said.

"Yes, I believe so. Here's a laugh! He asked if I could teach him what I know about riding and caring for a horse. I suggested that he talk to you. Maybe you can give him some pointers when you have time."

"Are you keeping up with your riding?"

"Not very well. In my spare time, I'm volunteering for H & H activities. But I did tell Louis that I'd ride with him tomorrow evening after I finish my work. You've been such a good teacher," she told him with a smile, "I can pass what you've taught me to Louis."

"Hot diggety dog!" Mason muttered under his

breath. Norah turned questioning eyes in his direction, but he glanced away.

The more she said, the more upset Mason became, and he stared out over the prairie. Why hadn't he spoken before this man came around? He'd been miserable the few days he'd been away from Norah, and he'd made up his mind that he couldn't let her leave him. But he'd decided to wait until summer was over, and if his affection for Norah kept increasing, he'd ask her to marry him. Had he waited too long? Was she interested in this man? He didn't want her riding with Louis Masters, but he couldn't think of any principled way to discourage it.

When the silence became unusually long, Norah said, "Louis is a missionary, home on furlough for a few months, and I've asked him for advice about the way to proceed with my plans. He thinks if I go ahead with my education, the way will open for me. But I can't go to school without money. And if I have to work to pay my way through college, it will take even longer for my preparation. If I could sell my house in Missouri, I'd have the funds I need."

Funny, Norah thought, that she wouldn't discuss her financial situation with Louis, but she was always pouring out her problems to Mason.

Wearily, Mason stood up. "I hope things work out for you, Norah," he said, and he meant it sincerely. He wouldn't stand in her way of doing what she felt God wanted her to do. But he returned to the Flying K a discouraged man.

During the remaining two weeks of the therapy session, Mason didn't come to the Bar 8 at all in the evenings. He occasionally came to observe the activities of H & H in the early morning, but he didn't visit the ranch house.

To avoid Louis, rather than to sit on the porch, Norah went to her room as soon as she finished the kitchen work. She believed that Louis was a fine man, but he wasn't Mason, and she didn't want to encourage his friendship.

"Have you and Mason quarreled?" Sheila asked one day as they were preparing dinner.

"No."

"Is he jealous of Louis Masters?" Sheila persisted.

"He has no reason to be."

"Mason is a sensitive man, and he might have decided he was getting in your way. He's also keen enough to know that Louis is more refined than he is—that you have the same interests."

Norah continued chopping onions for the casserole she was preparing, wondering if the tears in her eyes were from the onions.

"Doug says Mason is awful grouchy."

"Sheila, there's nothing between Mason and me,

so please don't try to make more of our relationship then there is."

"Okay, if you say so."

Mason didn't know why he was staying away from Norah. Just because she sat on the porch talking with Louis Masters, and had taken a few horseback rides around the corral with him, didn't give Mason any reason to avoid her. He'd had no idea how deeply he looked forward to her company until he didn't talk to her for a few days. Was he in love with Norah? He thought it wouldn't take long for him to love her, if he knew how she felt about him.

Although they would usually have spent weekends together, he was busy in the hay field now, wanting to get his hay baled before it rained. He worked until almost dark, so it wasn't easy to go see her, when she needed to go to bed early. But he could have at least stopped in to see her when he'd gone to watch the young riders. He excused his actions, rationalizing that mornings were her busiest times. He couldn't even bring himself to telephone in the evening, justifying his neglect by believing that when he came in from work, she'd be in bed. He couldn't understand what possessed him.

Finally, when he'd gotten so miserable he couldn't stay away, he drove to the Bar 8 and wandered into the kitchen where Sheila and Norah were working.

Trying to act naturally, as if no constraint lay between them, he said as he opened the screen door, "Got a cup of coffee for a hardworking man?"

Norah's heartbeat quickened, and she dared not look at him right away. "Sure thing. Pull up to the counter and pour yourself a cup."

"I just remembered," Sheila said, skittering around like a scared rabbit, "that I forgot to take Doug's jeans out of the dryer. I have to go home and fold them. Be back in a minute."

Mason poured a cup of coffee and there was a moment of stunned silence until they heard Sheila's car speeding away from the ranch house.

"That wasn't very subtle," Norah said, her embarrassment gone. "Sheila thinks you're avoiding me. Are you?" she added.

"I've been busy in the hay fields every day. This is a rancher's life, sometimes working from sunup till dark."

Norah took two cakes from the oven and drizzled a glaze over the top. She cut a large piece of the chocolate cake, placed it before Mason, and filled his coffee cup. She sat on the stool opposite him and nibbled on some carrot sticks.

"I've missed seeing you, Norah. I'll be working

all day Saturday, but maybe we can go out for dinner on Sunday."

"If you've been working hard all week, you'll want to stay at home Sunday. Would you like for me to come to the Flying K and prepare our meal there?"

"I'd love it! But you cook all week," Mason protested. "You need a break, too."

She shook her head. "No problem. I'll even ride over on Daisy to show you that I'm improving my riding skills."

Mason stood diffidently when it was time for him to leave. How far had things gone between her and Louis? Would he be overstepping his bounds to kiss her? Regardless, it had been too long since he'd had his arms around Norah, so he rounded the counter and pulled her upward into his arms. She buried her face against his throat, loving the feel of his soft skin next to hers. Even as he kissed her, Norah's lips spread into a smile.

"What's so funny?" he asked.

"Without your whiskers, I feel like a different man is kissing me. I like the new you."

"No, it's the same man—one who's missed being with you for too long and will count the minutes until Sunday."

Chapter Twelve

When Louis returned to the Bar 8 with the third group of children, he purposefully pursued Norah, which upset her more than it should have. He asked to speak to her privately on Thursday evening, and she prayed that Mason wouldn't show up while Louis was there.

She invited him into the house, rather than sitting on the porch. A strong southwest wind was making life miserable for humans and animals alike. Louis took Norah's hand.

"Sit beside me here on the couch. I have some serious things to say to you."

"I really wish you wouldn't. It's not the right time."

"I've known you less than a month, so perhaps

it *is* a little soon, but there's so much to be done for the salvation of the world, and so little time to do it that I can't delay.''

Norah tried to remove her hand from his, but he held on tightly.

''Norah, I'm asking you to marry me.''

When she started to remonstrate with him, he placed a finger on her lips.

''Hear me out. I know I'm springing this on you rather quickly, but I've given it a great deal of thought and prayer. I'm leaving for Africa in November, and I want you to go with me. As my wife, you wouldn't need a mission appointment, and you'd be a valuable asset to our mission station. As my wife, you can fulfill your lifetime dream.''

Protesting, Norah said, ''But, Louis, I hardly know you. I don't love you.''

''I understand that. I don't feel that I love you yet, either, but love will come. We have so much in common that it seems a perfect match. I've dreaded the thoughts of returning to my post alone, but with you at my side, I'll go gladly. Don't turn me down until you've thought about it.''

Norah's throat constricted, her lips trembled and she was afraid she would start crying. She should be rejoicing that the way was clear at last for her to be a missionary. If that was so, why did she feel so hollow inside, as if all the light had gone out of her world?

"I'll think about it," she struggled to say and sat as rigid as stone when Louis leaned over and kissed her softly on the lips.

"I'll be leaving tomorrow, and I hope you'll have an answer for me soon."

What could she do? If Louis was an objectionable person, it would be easy to say no. But he was a fine man, and she believed he would be a kind, considerate husband. But she didn't love him.

Norah turned off the downstairs lights and went upstairs. She drew the bath, and soaked in the tub until the water was lukewarm. She rubbed her body with a soothing lotion and went to the bedroom. Her heart was troubled, and she reached for the Bible— the only place she hoped to find an answer.

She needed the direction of the Holy Spirit more than she'd ever needed it before. In this case, it wasn't a decision between good or bad, for to go with Louis to the mission field would certainly be a good thing. Should she refuse him for no reason other than her confused feelings toward Mason?

Norah found two Scriptures that seemed to fit her particular situation, but they brought no joy to her heart. One passage in particular dealt with the cost of following Jesus. Jesus had approached a man about following him, and the would-be disciple had answered, "I will follow you, Lord, but first let me go back and say goodbye to my family."

Was Norah Williamson being like that man? *I'll follow you, Lord,* but...*let me follow at my own convenience*...but *let me follow by choosing the place where I'll serve*...but *let me follow with Mason instead of Louis.*

Jesus's answer to the man brought condemnation to Norah's heart. "No one who puts his hand to the plow and looks back is fit for service in the kingdom of God."

Usually, reading the Scriptures was encouraging to Norah, sending her to bed with a peace of mind that brought sleep speedily. But not so tonight. She lay awake for hours as the faces of Mason and Louis flashed back and forth in her mind's eye. She knew that her feelings for Mason had progressed beyond mere friendship, but never having been in love, she couldn't determine if she felt for Mason the deep-seated, fervent love that would last for a lifetime.

Nor did she know for sure that Mason loved her. It would be foolish to turn down an opportunity to serve on the mission field because of Mason, when she didn't even know how he felt about her. His few kisses had played havoc with her emotional equilibrium, but did they originate from a heart of love? Who could she ask what love was like? Sheila? No doubt the young woman would have plenty of advice, but Norah couldn't discuss this situation with anyone.

Although she wasn't a weepy woman, Norah cried herself to sleep when there seemed to be no answer from God.

Norah and Mason went riding on Sunday afternoon, and Mason could easily detect that Norah was preoccupied. She didn't show her obvious enjoyment of the prairie as she usually did. She stared straight ahead, speaking only when he asked her a direct question.

When they came to a lake, Mason said, "The deer have made a nice trail around this lake. It's about a mile long. Feel up to a walk?"

"Yes, why not? I'm not getting enough exercise, and it's showing in my waistline."

"I don't know why you worry about your weight. A lot of men, including me, don't prefer women who're thin as a rail. Ranch women are usually too busy to count calories. As long as you're healthy, a few extra pounds don't hurt anything."

It was good to know that Mason was pleased with her physical appearance, but that still didn't mean he had any long-term plans for her in his life. Would she have to tell him about Louis's proposal to find out?

Mason took off his boots and put on a pair of

walking shoes that he carried in his saddle bags before they started around the path. The crystal-blue
lake was surrounded by one of the largest sand
dunes in the state, where lush grasses intermingled
with stands of conifers. A few red cedar skeletons
stood against the skyline, and Norah looked upward
at the squeal of a red-tailed hawk expertly riding the
air currents above them. A ground squirrel beside
the path also heard the hawk's call, and he darted
into his burrow. They walked silently, each en-
grossed in their own thoughts, quietly enjoying nature. At the end of the circular trail, Norah leaned
against Daisy, her arms folded over the saddle.

"Louis asked me to marry him and accompany
him when he goes back to Africa in November."

After the first shock waves riffled through his
body, Mason said, "So that's why you're moody
today." It was something he'd feared—a situation
he wasn't ready to deal with today.

"Yes, it's constantly on my mind. I can't think
of anything else."

"Are you going to say yes?"

"I don't know—my mind's in a quandary. It
seems like a golden opportunity to do what God
called me to do when I was a girl."

His heart was beating at a rapid rate, and Mason
could hardly stand the suspense. The thought of her
being held in another man's arms weakened him,

and he leaned against his mount for support. In that moment, when he was on the verge of losing Norah, Mason finally realized that he loved her. He'd found a woman to love, one to fill the lonely hours of his life, but she was a woman who'd pledged her life to a special service to God. How could he ask her to stay with him when this might be the opportunity she'd wanted? Without looking at her, Mason said, "Then why are you hesitating?"

"I don't know Louis well enough to make such a decision, for one thing." He could feel her eyes looking at him. "What do you think I should do?" she asked pointedly.

This was his opportunity. Perhaps if he said, "Stay here with me," she'd accept. But would she live to regret it? She'd adjusted slowly to the Sand Hills region in good weather. And winter in this area was really the test of a person's adaptability to the environment.

The hardest thing Mason had ever done was to keep his voice from betraying his blighted hopes, and to say, "That's a question I can't answer for you. All you can do is ask God to guide you and follow His leading. If you make a decision not in keeping with God's will, you'll never be happy. I'll pray for you to make the right choice."

"Thanks, Mason." It was obvious to Norah that making her decision wouldn't be too hard. Mason didn't seem to mind that she would marry another man and step out of his life completely. So it wouldn't be a decision between Louis and Mason, but whether or not she wanted to take Louis up on his offer.

On Saturday, Norah was on her way home from grocery shopping in Valentine when she noted the signs of an impending storm. The day had been hot and humid, with practically no wind. Large clouds appeared in the sky, and she heard thunder in the distance, accompanied by a cloud that became dark and dense. Rounded masses at the bottom of the cloud twisted sinuously.

The storm had spawned a tornado! She needed to take cover, and she was several miles from home. She'd always been taught to try and outrun a tornado by traveling in an opposite direction from the way the storm was moving, but she couldn't determine the storm's route.

If she couldn't take cover, she should either lie flat on the ground or in a ravine, but as she turned off the highway toward the Flying K, it seemed as if the tornado was going away from her, so she accelerated the car, hoping to reach the ranch and Mason. The wind from the storm was so strong that it buffeted her small auto like a skiff tossed on the ocean waves.

Mason had taken the two dogs to the storm cellar, and when he saw Norah turn into his driveway, he raced to her.

"I've never been so happy to see anyone in my life," he cried as he jerked open the door of her car. "Sheila telephoned that you might be out in the storm. Hurry. We'll have to go to the storm cellar."

He took Norah's hand and pulled her from the car. Still holding her hand, he started running, almost jerking Norah off her feet as he raced behind the house. Lightning flashed, heavy rain and hail began to fall. A tree limb blew past and struck them, breaking Mason's stride. A hissing sound increased to a loud roar, but he rushed ahead to a set of steps that led into a small underground room, lit now by a propane lantern. The two dogs were whining and cowering in a corner.

With difficulty, Mason closed the slanted door against the sucking wind, hooked it from the inside and gathered Norah into his arms.

"Don't promise to marry Louis Masters just yet," he shouted above the clamor of the storm. "I love you, Norah. I didn't know how much until I thought you might be caught out in this storm. I don't want you to go against God's will for your life, but maybe there's another way."

Norah snuggled into his cozy embrace, and in spite of the storm over their heads, she felt secure.

"All right, Mason, I won't be hasty about it."

The noise over their heads was horrendous, until suddenly there was a terrible calm.

"That's when it's ready to strike," Mason said, as he stood and paced around the small room. The ceiling was so low that his head was only an inch from the top. "I may lose everything I have."

Norah took his hand, and she encouraged him to sit on a cot that had a thin mattress on it.

Hoping to divert his attention, she said, "Are there many tornadoes here? Do you have to use the storm cellar often?"

He sat at Norah's side, clutching her hand so tightly that her fingers numbed, but she suffered the discomfort in silence. Whining, the dogs curled up at their feet, and Mason soothed them with a few words.

"When I was a child, before we had radar to track storms, I spent many nights in the cellar. If the weather was stormy, Dad would grab some blankets, pick me up out of bed and bring me down here. Sometimes I wouldn't even wake up. Once I was safe, he'd sit on the porch and watch the skies."

"It's a dry place to wait out a storm."

Norah was no stranger to tornadoes, because many passed through Missouri, and she mentioned a time or two when tornadoes had struck close to their home.

"We've never had much damage on the Flying K, but I'm afraid this time we will have." He stood and walked toward the door. "I imagine the storm is past now, so I might as well see what's happened."

He lifted the door, stood on the steps and peered out. It was raining, and the wind was blustery, but the thunder and lightning had receded into the distance. Mason said nothing, and Norah went to stand beside him.

"Well?"

"The barn is gone!"

"Oh, Mason."

He climbed the steps. "The house looks all right, though. Come on up if you want to. I can see the storm to the northeast, so you'll be safe in the house. Leave the dogs down here for the time being."

The yard was white with large pieces of hail, and the wind from the northwest was several degrees colder than it had been before the storm. Twisted timbers and scattered bales of hay were scattered where the huge barn had been before, but the silo stood intact. The barn roof was lying a half mile away in the pasture.

"Go in the house, Norah. I'm going to look around and see what other damage there is."

"Let me come with you."

Mason nodded and held out his hand. Oblivious

to the rain that drenched her clothing, she clasped his hand as he walked among the buildings. Stripped of their leaves, the trees were as bare as they'd be in winter. Twisted limbs were scattered among the other debris. Mason ran toward the two cottonwood trees that had been planted by his grandmother. One of them was split from top to bottom, and at its base lay six cattle.

"It's Buster," Norah said sadly, noting the Hereford bull lifeless on the ground.

"Yes," Mason said in a low, tormented voice. "I guess he won't scare you again." Norah shuddered at the anguish on his face.

Tears came to Norah's eyes. She'd long ago gotten over her fear of the bull and had come to regard him with some nostalgia, since he'd been responsible for her dramatic meeting with Mason. Seeing him lying there was like losing an old friend.

"I'll go to the house and fix some coffee," she said, thinking he might want to be alone for a while.

He nodded. "Get the cell phone from my truck and see if you can contact Doug or Sheila. I want to know if there's been any damage at the Bar 8. I'm sure glad the kids are gone for the weekend."

As she walked toward the house, Norah marveled that Mason's truck and her car hadn't been damaged, but it seemed the tornado had only touched down in the barn area. She found the phone and dialed Doug's cell phone.

"We've been worried about you," he said when Norah said hello. "Thank God you're all right and able to talk on the phone."

"I know enough about prairie storms to take shelter. How are things at the Bar 8?"

"We're okay," Doug said, "but I thought the storm was hanging close to the Flying K. Any problems?"

"Lots of them. The barn is gone, and at least six cattle were killed."

"We'll come right over," Doug said.

She turned from the phone when Mason entered the room. "Everything's all right at the Bar 8."

Mason's shoulders were stooped more than usual, and he walked as if he were in a trance. As she prepared the coffeemaker, Norah asked, "Did you find any other damage?"

"The roof is ruined on the machinery shed, but thanks to God, none of the machinery is destroyed. It could have been much worse."

Heaving a deep sigh, he sat at the table and stretched out his legs. Norah stood behind him and massaged his neck and shoulders. He closed his eyes and surrendered his strong body to the soothing strokes of her hands, slowly feeling at peace with the damage to his property. But what if he'd had to endure the storm and its aftermath alone? What if, at the end of the summer, Norah left the Bar 8 and he hadn't done anything about it? What if Norah married Louis Masters and went to Africa?

"You'll never know how much your company has meant to me today," he said. "When I thought you might have been caught in the storm, I was scared out of my wits. After these months together, I can't imagine a life without you. I meant what I said in the cellar. Let's forget all the 'ifs and ands' and get married."

Before she could answer, a truck door slammed, and Doug and Sheila ran into the house. Feeling deflated, Norah dropped her hands and moved away from Mason's chair.

"At least the two of you are safe," Sheila said, tears in her eyes. "Doug was watching, and when the funnel lifted, black with debris, he was sure it had hit the Flying K."

"Have you heard if anyone else had any damage?" Mason asked.

"Except for some minor hail and wind damage, our folks' ranches are all right," Sheila said.

"The way the tornado headed, I figure it missed the other ranches nearby, but it's a bad storm. It'll probably touch down again," Doug said.

Mason lifted himself from the chair. "Come on. You might as well see what's happened," he said.

"I'll have some sandwiches ready when you get back," Norah said.

"I'll stay and help Norah. I've already seen enough tornado aftermath in my life."

"Here's some leftover roast beef in the refrigerator," Norah said, checking out Mason's supplies. "If you'll slice that for sandwiches, I'll prepare an apple cobbler and pop it in the oven. We can serve it warm with milk or ice cream on it. Mason needs all the coddling he can get right now."

Sheila nodded as she opened a loaf of bread. "Doug's worried about him. Most ranchers can't afford to carry the coverage they need, so he probably won't receive enough insurance to pay for the barn. Mason has had a few financial reverses the past two years. That's the reason he's selling the Bar 8."

"Jim Hanson hoped H & H could operate here again next year."

Sheila shook her head. "Not much chance of that. Mason is between a rock and a hard place. He'll have to sell."

Sheila's words were the proverbial straw that broke the camel's back. To Norah, it seemed as though every time she began to think of a possible future with Mason, something happened to ruin it.

Chapter Thirteen

With the final week of the therapeutic project under way, Norah didn't have time to keep up with Mason's tornado damage. He didn't come to the Bar 8, and they had only a few conversations by phone. She avoided Louis as much as possible.

On Thursday night, when Mason came for the campfire meeting, Jim Hanson asked to speak to him after the children were housed in the dormitory. Norah invited them into the house for their conference.

Jim and Mason sat at one of the tables in the dining room. Norah made a pot of coffee and placed it between them. While they talked, she put away the picnic utensils, and from the gist of their conversation, she was sure she wouldn't be using them again.

"This summer's project has been so successful," Jim said, "that the board of directors wanted me to find out if we can continue using the Bar 8 for our program. Instead of three months, they want to plan a six months' program next year, extending the program to adults with disabilities. They'll need an answer within the next few weeks."

"I can give you the answer now," Mason said. "I plan to sell the Bar 8 if I can find a buyer. The Realtor is advertising it again next week."

"That's really disappointing to us, Mr. King."

"It's a disappointment to me, too. I liked having you here, but I can't afford to keep the Bar 8. It's never been a good investment, and I've used income from the Flying K to pay the mortgage on this place. If it hadn't been for the tornado, I might have held on a little longer, but I don't have enough insurance to cover the cost of rebuilding my barn. I have to sell."

Jim shook hands with him. "I do understand, Mr. King, but it's been a great setup for us, even if it hasn't been for you. Thanks very much."

After Jim left, Norah went into the dining room where Mason sat, turning his coffee cup round and round on the tabletop, staring at the floor. She sat across from him.

"I feel lower than a snake," he said. "After seeing how the therapeutic program has benefited these kids, I want to help them. But my back is to the wall, and I have to sell the Bar 8 or lose the Flying K. That's my ancestral heritage—I can't risk losing it.''

Norah reached across the table and took one of his hands. ''God knows you want to help, and He understands why you can't. You've already sacrificed one summer for the H & H. Don't worry about it.''

''That's not the only thing that worries me. What are you going to do? Will you be leaving?''

Norah left the table and walked to the window, staring out into the darkness.

''I don't know what to do. I had thought this summer's activity was a perfect setting to receive an insight into what my future should be. If anything, I'm more unsettled now than I was before I left Missouri.''

''Are you going to accept Masters's proposal?''

''Do you think I should?''

Mason hadn't mentioned again his impulsive marriage proposal on the day of the tornado. How could he answer such a question? Mason wanted to shout ''No,'' but in all fairness to Norah, he didn't think he should influence her decision. If God had called Norah to the mission field, he wouldn't stand in her way. But how could he stand aside and let her marry anyone other than himself? Still, with his current financial problems, what did he have to offer her?

Mason cleared his throat, saying slowly, "It seems like a good way for you to fulfill your dream of being a missionary. Married to him, you could be on the mission field before Christmas."

Norah's heart plummeted, wishing that Mason was more like the mythical knight who grabbed his sweetheart, threw her over his saddle and rode away with her. If Mason would do that, she wouldn't have to make the decision. But she could understand why Mason was leaving the decision up to her.

"Yes, that's true."

"Then you're going to marry him?"

"I'll have to think about it," Norah said, as if she hadn't been fretting about it for weeks.

Louis stayed on after breakfast the next morning and asked to speak to Norah privately. Sheila hurried out of the kitchen.

Louis came close to Norah and held her hand. "I need my answer. I've been praying that it will be the answer I want."

She walked away from him and faced him. "I have no answer, Louis. Since I'm not accepting your proposal wholeheartedly, I consider that a red flag to say no."

"I won't take no for an answer," he persisted. "I can't understand your hesitation—you told me that you've wanted to be a missionary since you were a teenager. I'm giving you an opportunity to fulfill that dream. Your responsibilities end here today, and I can't think of any other reason why you won't accept me.''

Norah could think of a reason—a big six-foot-plus reason, but she couldn't tell Louis she wanted to stay with Mason. Except for that impulsive proposal at the ranch on the day the tornado struck, he hadn't given her any reason to think he wanted her. But regardless of her wish to be a missionary, and even if Mason didn't renew his proposal, it would be making a mockery of marriage to marry a man she didn't love.

''No,'' she said, shaking her head.

''Will you take another week to think it over and telephone me your answer? It's a perfect setup for both of us. I need a companion, you need a way to the mission field. It's an ideal situation.''

''I've always dreamed that I'd someday have a love-filled marriage—not one of convenience.''

Louis covered the space between them in a few seconds and took her in his arms. But she drew away when he bent to kiss her.

''Love will come, Norah. Love will follow.''

When her heart was untouched where he was concerned, she knew love would never follow with Louis. But she did agree to delay the decision.

''I'll take another week to consider.''

*   *   *

Norah hadn't had any anxiety attacks about darkness for weeks, but now that she knew she'd not be living here again, the house seemed very quiet that evening. She kept wishing Mason would telephone, but when he didn't, she dialed his number about ten o'clock.

"Do you mind if I leave my things at the Bar 8 for a few days?" she said. "I know I'm no longer employed by you, but I want some time alone where no one knows me. I've made arrangements to go to Mahoney State Park near Omaha for a couple of days. I'll be back Monday, hopefully, with all my questions answered."

"I don't have a buyer for the Bar 8 yet, so stay as long as you want to," Mason said, wishing she could be there all the time.

Since the major vacation months had passed, Norah had looked forward to a quiet environment at the state park, but when she telephoned for reservations, she was surprised that the lodge was completely booked for the days she wanted to be there. However, as she spoke to the reservations clerk, a cancelation had just been made, and she was able to book a room. She assumed that senior citizens took advantage of the fall season to rest in the spacious lodge, visit the air force museum adjacent to the park and enjoy the natural beauty of the area.

Norah's mind wasn't on sightseeing. She wanted some solitude to sort out the conflicting thoughts that were destroying her peace of mind. She had to make some decisions.

On her drive from Valentine to Omaha, for her own safety on the highway, Norah determined to get her mind off the dilemma she faced. She felt a desperate need to hear God's word, and since she couldn't read the Bible and drive at the same time, she played a tape of the Bible. Asking God to lead her to a portion of the Bible to calm her inner turmoil, she settled on Psalm 145, which she repeated over and over as she drove. Although she'd been a Christian for years, during the hours she was on the road, Norah learned many new insights into her relationship with God. When she fixed her mind on the greatness of God, everything else in her life faded into the background.

The psalmist had first of all praised God. ''Every day I will praise You and extol Your name for ever and ever,'' David had written. And certain other verses wended their way into Norah's mind, words that she mentally stored up for future use. ''The Lord is faithful to all His promises and loving toward all He has made.''

But the verse that encouraged Norah more than

any other was, "The Lord is near to all who call on Him, to all who call on Him in truth. He fulfills the desires of those who fear Him; He hears their cry and saves them."

Norah asked God to forgive her for not trusting Him for leadership, and she believed sincerely that before this weekend was over, she'd have the answer to her vexing problem. As she parked at Mahoney, she walked into the lodge with a lighter heart than she'd had for months. God was in control of her life, and she'd made herself available to His leading.

Norah's room was on the second floor, with a balcony that overlooked the Platte River Valley.

After she unpacked the few clothes she'd brought and laid out her toiletries, Norah sat on the balcony for over an hour hoping that in this quiet place, she'd receive some insight into the decision she should make. Although she prayed for guidance, she didn't receive an answer. She seemed detached from her immediate problems and grew restless.

She didn't want to talk to anyone, so Norah went into the dining room and bought a slice of pizza to take to her room. She flipped on the television while she ate, not really interested in any of the programs she watched. She couldn't remember when she'd spent a more boring evening. She went to bed only to toss and turn most of the night. When morning came, she knew for her own peace of mind that she had to make a decision soon.

After a substantial breakfast, she spent the morning walking briskly along the trail that led to the Platte River. A few colorful leaves heralded the beginning of the autumn season, Norah's favorite time of the year.

Contemplating the fact that she'd entered the autumn season of her life, Norah suddenly believed that even if she was in the mellow years, the most beautiful time of her life was yet to come. Were those years to be spent with Mason or Louis? She knew what *she* wanted, but this morning, as she enjoyed God's creation and praised Him, she submitted her will to His.

Back at the lodge, she stopped at the snack bar to buy a sandwich and soda, which she took back to her room. She sat on the balcony, enjoying the warmth of the afternoon.

She had dallied long enough. This was decision time. Crunch time. She remembered the words of Joshua when he'd told the Hebrew people, "Why halt you between two opinions?" Surely God must be saying the same thing to her.

She had several decisions to make, and it was right that she be alone to make them, rather than in the Sand Hills, where thoughts of Mason were ever present.

Did God want her to be a missionary in a foreign country? If so, should she marry Louis Masters as a way of responding to God's call? Should she marry a man she didn't love? Or should she enroll in college and reach her goal the hard way—by four or five years of intensive study and preparation?

Those questions were difficult enough, but when she considered her feelings for Mason, she wondered if she'd misread God's call. She loved Mason, but she wondered if he loved her, or was his interest in her just physical attraction? If he did ask her to marry him, was he doing so out of love or simply because he was lonely? She loved him, so should she marry him regardless of his reason for asking?

In her youth, when she'd been so disappointed that she had to stay home and take care of her family rather than go to the mission field, she'd gone to her pastor for counseling. She'd never forgotten one thing he'd said to her. "The light that shines the longest distance, shines the brightest at home."

He'd explained to her that her concern for the lost in overseas countries, would enable her to see what needed to be done in her own home and community. She'd accepted his counsel to serve in the place God had placed her. And, except for rare moments of rebellion, she'd willingly done what she knew she should do.

Was it possible that God still wanted her to be a

missionary in her own country? She'd felt spiritually fulfilled this summer volunteering with H & H, cooking for the children, helping them work with the horses and singing with Mason and the Johnsons to entertain the kids. She'd daydreamed about marrying Mason and continuing the work with H & H, thinking this would fulfill her missionary longings. She had been practically settled in her mind that she could continue to do such work and still be in God's will, when Louis Masters came to the Bar 8.

But even if Louis hadn't entered the picture, now that the tornado had made it necessary for Mason to sell the Bar 8, she wouldn't be able to continue work with H & H. She couldn't lull herself into believing that simply marrying Mason and living in the Sand Hills would in any way fulfill Christ's command to His disciples to ''go and make disciples of all nations, baptizing them in the name of the Father and of the Son and of the Holy Spirit, and teaching them to obey everything I have commanded you.''

Having submitted her will completely to God, Norah wasn't as concerned about these questions as she had been yesterday, for she was convinced now that the answer would come. She showered, changed into dress slacks and a blouse, and made her way to the dining room. The lobby and entrance to the restaurant were overflowing with people, and the hubbub was deafening. She started to turn back, believing she'd never find a table, when the head waiter saw her hesitation. He motioned Norah forward and took her to a small table near a window where she would have a pleasant view.

"Most of the dining room has been reserved for a special party," he explained, "but we have a few tables for our other guests. It may be a little noisy, but I hope you won't mind. We're closing the dining room at nine when they want to have a program, but you'll have plenty of time for dinner."

Pulling out a chair and seating her, he handed her a menu. "Do you want the buffet tonight?"

She shook her head. "Just a bowl of vegetable soup and salad. And a cup of hot tea after I've eaten."

At least a hundred people had converged on the dining room about the time Norah's soup was served. She concentrated on her food, but she couldn't avoid awareness of the other guests as they gathered around the buffet line. The majority of them were of Native American descent.

When she realized she was the only guest other than the special party, Norah ate her food hurriedly. She was curious about the gathering, but she didn't want to intrude on their festivities, so she decided to return to her room. She signaled the waitress and canceled her order for tea.

Her remark must have been overheard, for a distinguished-looking man approached her. "Ma'am, we apologize for ruining your dinner. I know we're noisy, but this is a special occasion, and since you're alone, why not join us? I'm Smith Eagleton. We're honoring a woman who has served the Sioux nation for years. It would be our privilege to have you stay with us."

He nodded toward a short, wizened, gray-haired woman, apparently the guest of honor.

Norah believed his invitation was sincere, and since she wanted to put off her personal decision a little longer, she agreed to stay. Smith Eagleton brought her a piece of cake and a cup of tea.

Apparently master of ceremonies for the evening, Smith soon stepped up on a platform and called the group to order.

"We're here tonight to pay tribute to Emma Curtis, who came to the Sioux Reservation as a missionary schoolteacher sixty years ago. She's had a tremendous impact on hundreds of Sioux children, setting our feet on the right path as she taught us our ABCs."

The program continued as several men and women, who'd prospered in the business world, reported that they owed their success to Miss Emma's guidance. The shy little woman was finally brought to the platform where she was given a large album filled with letters from her former students.

The climax of the program came when Smith said, "Two years ago, Miss Emma retired from active teaching and went to live with her sister. Now her sister has died, and Miss Emma has no home. So, out of respect for Miss Emma and the life she dedicated to our people, we've established a foundation in her honor, the proceeds of which will pay her expenses to live in a retirement community of her choice. When the day comes that Miss Emma no longer needs the income, the money will be invested in a scholarship fund in her memory, the proceeds to help deserving Sioux youth attend college."

Miss Emma was an agile octogenarian, and during the applause, she walked briskly to the podium and took the microphone from the emcee.

"What a fuss!" she said sternly in her best teacher's voice. "I've a notion to make all of you stand in the corner."

Loud laughter greeted her remark, but when she said quietly into the microphone, "That's enough. Let me have your attention," the group quieted down quickly. The teacher had spoken!

Clutching the large album, containing accolades from former students, in her fragile arms, Miss Emma gave a great smile. "Perhaps now's the time to tell you that I came reluctantly to the reservation. For you see, I didn't want to be a schoolteacher. I wanted to enter the convent, but my parents absolutely refused to let me become a nun. For years, it's been a disappointment to me that I didn't get to do what I believed God had called me to do. But as I look back over my life, I realize that God sent me where I was supposed to be. As your teacher, I've impacted many more lives than I would have reached in the cloister. And I have been happy.''

Miss Emma's words hit Norah hard like a slap in the face, and she slipped quietly from the dining hall.

Norah walked to her room as dazed as if she were walking in her sleep. Was this her answer? Stunned by the similarity of Miss Emma's situation and her own, Norah wondered if God was trying to tell her that her dedication to the mission field was *her* idea not His will for her life.

Oh, God, if this is true, then I don't have to hesitate any longer. If Mason knows that You've set me free from my youthful vow, surely he'll ask me to marry him. Is it possible that I can find fulfillment for my life as Mason's wife?

Chapter Fourteen

An hour later, when she left her room to get a bucket of ice, Norah saw Miss Emma at the door across the hall, inserting a key into the lock. She looked up at Norah with keen blue eyes.

Impulsively, Norah reached out her hand and said, "I was in the dining room earlier. Congratulations on your long and satisfying career."

The blue eyes sparkled mischievously. "It wasn't always satisfying while I was teaching. We had lots of problems, but joys, too."

"Miss Emma," Norah said impulsively, "would you have time to talk with me tomorrow morning? I've come here to make some decisions about my future, and since part of your situation parallels mine, it would be helpful if I could talk to you."

"I'll be leaving early in the morning, but I'll talk with you now."

"Oh, but it's so late. I shouldn't bother you."

"No bother at all. I've always been a night owl. I'll not go to bed for another hour or so." She opened her door. "Come on in."

With Miss Emma holding her hand, Norah told her everything—of her missionary call, the years she'd stayed with her family, her work with H & H, Louis's proposal and her love for Mason.

Miss Emma chuckled. "It's obvious you can't do all of those things. What do you want to do?"

"More than anything else, I want to do what God wants me to do, but I'd like to do that and have Mason, too."

Miss Emma looked at her with complete understanding. "It took a long time for me to finally comprehend that *every* Christian is a missionary. God has a mission field for all of us—it might be in your own neighborhood, or maybe on the other side of the world, but He expects us to serve where we are."

"I believe that, too," Norah said. "In fact, my pastor said similar words to me when I had to give up my college plans to help at home."

"I often think about the prophet Jonah, who ran away from his call when God told him to preach to the people of Nineveh. But the Ninevites were Jonah's enemies, and he rebelled against God's call.''

''I've not really been rebellious,'' Norah said slowly, ''but I haven't always served willingly.''

Miss Emma patted Norah's shoulder. ''My situation exactly, and, like Jonah, it took a while to learn my lesson. His experience proves that God cares about every human being whether that person is a businessman in New York City, a rancher in Nebraska, a tribesman in the heart of Africa or children on a Sioux reservation. The whole world is a mission field.''

''How long did it take you to know that God wanted you on the reservation rather than in the convent?''

Amusement lit Miss Emma's eyes, and she giggled—a trait seemingly so out of character for the little woman, that it was endearing. ''Sixty years.''

''Then I still have a few years to learn what He wants to tell me,'' Norah said lightly, adapting herself to Miss Emma's mood.

''You obviously are a compassionate person or you wouldn't have taken care of your brother with love and tenderness. Or have given yourself wholeheartedly to the children who came to H & H this summer.''

Norah stood, walked slowly around the room,

looking for a moment out the window. "So our mission field is wherever we are."

"Right. There's no end to the needs of the world, but you're only one person. Jesus told His disciples, 'Look at the fields! They are ripe for harvest. The harvest is plentiful but the laborers are few. Ask the Lord of the harvest, therefore, to send out workers into His harvest field.'"

"I memorized that Scripture when I was a child. Jesus also told His disciples to pray that God would send laborers into His field. He said, 'Go! I'm sending you.' I believe that message was for me, too."

Miss Emma nodded approvingly. "And no doubt it was, but you can't go everywhere. If God wants you to marry Mason King and live in the Sand Hills, you'll find your mission field there. But if it seems that you're to marry the other fellow and go to Africa, you'll get over your feelings for Mason. Only you can decide, but you'll know when you make the right decision by the peace that comes to your heart."

Miss Emma laid her hand on Norah's head. "Your problem is that you expect your whole life's plan to be revealed before you act. Faith doesn't work that way. Sometimes we have to take one step at a time. Years ago, I came across a Bible verse that taught me to live by faith."

"My faith is weak, Miss Emma, so will you share the verse with me?"

"The message is very meaningful in a modern translation, 'I am the Lord your God, who teaches you what is best for you, who directs you in the way you should go.' Based on those words, I made up a little slogan that I repeat often when the way before me is obscure—'God knows best what is best for me.'"

"If you don't mind, I'd like to take that slogan for my own."

"I'd be honored to think I've given you something to affirm your faith in God."

Norah embraced Miss Emma's fragile shoulders. "I can understand why your former students honored you tonight," she said. "I've only known you a few hours and you've already been a blessing to me. You've made my decision easier."

Back in her room, Norah knelt beside the bed, her face resting on the pillow. It was humiliating to know that she'd spent most of her life fretting about things she should have accepted on faith. Hadn't Jesus once rebuked His disciples for their lack of faith?

When she couldn't remember the exact incident that had prompted Jesus's words to His disciples, she took her Bible and sat on the side of the bed. She soon found the passage where Jesus had questioned the faith of His disciples when they were in a boat crossing the Sea of Galilee. Jesus was asleep when a sudden storm threatened to capsize the boat. Frightened, the disciples awakened Jesus and asked Him if He didn't care that they were going to perish.

Norah read the rest of the story aloud in the poetic King James Version of the Bible.

''And He arose, and rebuked the wind, and said unto the sea, 'Peace, be still.' And the wind ceased, and there was a great calm.' And He said unto them, 'Why are ye so fearful? How is it that ye have no faith?' ''

Just as Jesus's words had calmed the disciples, peace flooded Norah's heart and mind. Her spirit was no longer filled with the roiling questions and doubts that had made her miserable for weeks. She laid aside the Bible, silently thanked God for showing her the way, got into bed and went to sleep.

After enjoying a restful night's sleep, Norah was awake when she heard Miss Emma's door open the next morning. Norah shrugged quickly into a robe and went into the hall. A small suitcase sat on the floor, and Miss Emma was locking the door. Norah handed her a piece of paper.

''Here's my name and a temporary address. Will you contact me when you're settled in your new home? Perhaps in your retirement years, you can mentor those of us who need help. I'd like to keep in touch with you.''

''Have you reached a decision?''

''I won't marry Louis. He lives in Omaha, and I intend to telephone him this morning. It still may be right for me to go to the mission field, but not as his wife.''

Miss Emma smiled. ''And your next step?''

''God hasn't revealed that yet, but, Lord willing, my intentions are to return to the Sand Hills today. I realize that I have to accept God's guidance daily, and not expect Him to give me a blueprint for the rest of my life. I'll meet each situation as it comes along. If I keep in close communion with God through Bible study and prayer, I believe He'll guide me daily.''

''I *know* He will,'' Miss Emma agreed. ''God bless you, Norah.''

''He already has! I've had a full life, but I didn't always recognize it as such. I'm sorry now that I didn't enjoy one day at a time without fretting about what might have been.''

Smith Eagleton came down the hallway and picked up Miss Emma's luggage. Norah waved goodbye as they walked away.

Since Louis had viewed the marriage as a convenience, rather than a love match, his heart wasn't involved, so the telephone conversation with him wasn't as painful as Norah had feared. He received her decision with equanimity, although he did voice his regrets that she wouldn't be working with him.

Once this was done, Norah moved to terminate the conversation, but Louis said, "I've wondered if your refusal stems from your interest in Mr. King. Are you in love with him?"

"Yes, I am, but I can honestly say that my love for Mason didn't influence my decision. I've asked God to work His will in my life, and I'm sorry, but I'm definitely convinced that doesn't include marriage to you. But I'll always appreciate the fact that you asked me."

Norah considered telephoning Mason and reporting her decision, but she preferred to tell him in person, so she packed quickly and checked out of the lodge. The miles seemed to drag by as she encountered more than one delay on the highway, and it was late afternoon before she turned off the highway to the Flying K property. She stopped in front of the ranch house, and her eagerness dropped to rock bottom when she realized the place was deserted.

She heard Pete and Repeat barking, and found them in their kennels behind the house. They whined piteously, and she took time to rub their heads. Mason's pickup was in the garage. When she walked toward the barn, she saw that Mason had apparently been clearing away the debris from the barn wreckage. He'd even destroyed the silo, although he'd hoped that he could build the new barn beside the undamaged silo.

Baffled, Norah drove on to the Bar 8, disappointed that she had to wait longer to see Mason. But the Bar 8 ranch seemed deserted, too. Where was everyone?

Norah realized that the quietness didn't stem from the absence of the children and the H & H vans that she'd grown accustomed to during the summer. Both of the Johnsons' vehicles were gone and no tractors or other equipment were visible.

The answering machine light was blinking when Norah went into the kitchen. With a trembling finger, she pushed the button for a message.

"Norah," Sheila's voice sounded, "I'm telephoning, Monday at noon. We're all at the Melham Memorial Hospital in Broken Bow. Mason was injured today while he was trying to clear away the tornado damage at the Flying K. The silo crumbled and fell on him. Call the hospital when you get home."

"God knows best what is best for me," Norah repeated over and over while her nervous fingers dialed the number Sheila had given and she waited until someone paged Sheila.

When Sheila reached the phone, considering her

rapid pulse rate, Norah said in a surprisingly calm voice, "This is Norah."

"We tried to telephone you at Mahoney's, but you'd already checked out," Sheila said in a strained voice.

"What happened?"

"Everyone thought the silo hadn't been damaged at all from the tornado, but apparently it had been. Mason was on the tractor today clearing away the debris of the barn, and the silo suddenly collapsed and fell on him. Doug's father was there helping, and he telephoned for help. There were twenty ranchers at the Flying K within a half hour. They uncovered Mason, or—" Sheila's voice trembled "—he'd have been buried alive."

"How is he?"

"He's alive—that's all we know."

"I'll leave immediately."

Sheila gave directions to the hospital, adding, "Be careful, Norah. Don't drive fast and do something foolish. He'll probably be all right. The ambulance was there by the time the neighbors had dug him out of the rubble. Little time was lost getting him to the hospital."

"See you soon."

To lessen her concern for Mason, as she used all her willpower to observe the speed limit on the drive to Broken Bow, Norah recalled what she'd learned from Miss Emma last night and repeated over and over, ''God knows best what is best for me.''

The streetlights were glowing when she drove into Broken Bow and up the hill to the hospital. When Norah stepped from her car and walked into the hospital on unsteady legs, the large United States flag was snapping in a northwest wind that also wafted the unmistakable smell of the nearby cattle feed lot.

A nurse directed her to the emergency room's waiting area where she found Sheila, Doug, and his parents, Paul and Mary.

I will not cry, Norah said mentally when Sheila ran to her. Norah put her arms around Sheila as she looked over her shoulder to Paul Johnson, whose worried countenance wasn't reassuring.

''What news is there?''

''Not much,'' Paul said. ''The doctor talked to us an hour ago. Mason is bruised all over, has several cracked ribs and his right hip is fractured. He's still unconscious, and the doctor is concerned about a blow to his head.''

''How long before they know anything about his recovery?''

Paul shook his head. ''Maybe not for days.''

''We've decided that some of us need to stay here,'' Doug said. ''We were getting ready to go to a motel and make reservations for the night. Do you want us to reserve a room for you?''

"No,'' Norah said. "I'll stay at the hospital the rest of the night. Someone should be here.''

"I'm staying,'' Paul Johnson said, "so you don't need to.''

"I'd prefer to stay until we know his condition. But I haven't eaten anything since morning, so I want to go and have dinner.''

"I'll go with you. Doug, why don't you and Sheila stay here until we've eaten?'' Paul said. "After we've had supper, I'll leave Mary at the motel, and she can make reservations for all of you.''

After they returned to the hospital, Paul and Norah settled down for a long night of waiting. The doctor came in again, and said that they should know by morning if Mason's head injury was merely a concussion or something more serious. No one else was in the waiting room, and Paul reminisced about his and Mason's younger days.

"We caused our parents a lot of worry,'' he said, "because we were both daredevils. We'd ride any horse that we saw. One summer we followed the rodeo circuit, and neither one of us ever broke a bone. And just to think that Mason was moving around peacefully on his tractor, and this happened to him.''

"He was counting on the stability of that silo. This will cause him more financial worry."

"That's true," Paul said absentmindedly, still thinking of the past. "I always felt sorry for Mason because he didn't have a mother. Mom took him under her wing, and he spent as much time at our ranch as he did at the Flying K.

"I was so happy for him when he found Cecily, and I thought he'd not be lonely anymore. But I sat right here in this hospital with Mason the time Cecily lost their boy and then died herself. In his agitation, he said he'd never risk another woman's life to bear his children."

Norah wasn't surprised, for it was similar to what Mason had told her.

"Mason became withdrawn after that," Paul continued, "and although eventually, he was more like his old self, I'd never seen him *really* happy again until this summer." He gave Norah a keen-eyed glance. "I suppose you know you're responsible for that."

Without meeting Paul's eyes, Norah fiddled with a button on her blouse, saying, "Has he told you so?"

"Didn't have to," Paul answered. "I know Mason well enough that he doesn't have to tell me things. What are your plans, Norah?"

"I went away for a couple of days to make a lot

of decisions," Norah said. "I won't go into detail now, but God taught me one big lesson—all I need to face the future is faith in Him. I've spent too much time depending on Norah Williamson, trying to work out my own life. I came back today, not knowing when I'd leave the Sand Hills, or even where I'd go if I did, but I came determined to move one day at a time. When I learn the extent of Mason's injury, I'll take the next step."

At intervals during the night, Paul and Norah went into the intensive care room where Mason lay, wan and still. Once, Norah kissed his forehead, but he had no response. The nurses assured them that his condition was stable, and they had to be content with that.

The rest of the Johnson family returned early in the morning, and having had their breakfast, insisted that Paul and Norah eat.

"I'll stop for breakfast on my way back to the ranch," Paul said. "And, Doug, you'd better go with me. We'll have three ranches to look after until Mason is back on his feet. But somebody needs to stay here."

"I'm not leaving until we know more about his condition," Norah said. "I still have the suitcase in the car that I took with me to Mahoney. I'll check into a motel. You all have work to do, but I'm available."

"I'll stay with you," Sheila added.

"Then you might as well go home with us, Mary," Paul said to his wife. "We can come back tonight."

By the time the doctor came into the waiting room at ten o'clock in the morning, Sheila and Norah had exhausted every subject they could think of and were sitting in silence.

"Mr. King has regained consciousness, and he's asking for Norah. Is that one of you?" he asked.

Norah sensed that her face had flushed, but she held up her hand.

"Come along, then. He's still woozy, but seeing you might calm him. For some reason, he's restless, and that isn't good for him right now."

Mason's eyes were turned toward the door when Norah and the doctor entered. A slight smile passed over his face. He was hooked up to so many machines, he couldn't lift his hands, so Norah laid her hand on his arm.

"When'd you get back?" he whispered.

She knew from this statement that he was lucid, and she silently thanked God for His mercy.

"Yesterday. I came to the hospital as soon as I heard."

"What happened to me? I feel like a ton of bricks fell on me."

"Not a ton of bricks—the silo."

"How badly am I hurt?"

The doctor answered his question. "You have some broken bones, and you're bruised all over. Nothing that won't mend, but it may take a while."

"Sheila's in the waiting room—do you want to see her?" Norah asked.

"No more visitors right now," the doctor interjected. "And it's time for you to go, too."

Norah nodded assent. Mason's eyes turned bleak at the prospect of her absence, and she smoothed back his hair. "Sheila and I are staying in Broken Bow until you're better."

"Norah?" he asked weakly, an unspoken question in his voice.

"Before I left Mahoney's yesterday morning, I telephoned Louis and told him I wouldn't accept his offer. Is that what you want to know?"

"Yes," he whispered.

"Then try to rest. I'm staying here as long as you need me."

Chapter Fifteen

Since Mason was going to be in the intensive care unit for a few days, and Norah could only see him for short periods, she left Sheila to look after Mason while she went to the Bar 8 for items she'd need for an extended stay in a motel. When Mason was moved into a semiprivate room, and the doctor assured them that he would recover completely, Sheila went home.

Norah went to the hospital each day in midmorning and stayed until closing hours at night. Since they had no privacy, Norah and Mason couldn't talk of the things that mattered most to them. He was taking pain medication, and he slept a good part of the day. When he opened his eyes and saw Norah sitting beside the bed, reading or crocheting, Mason smiled contentedly and went back to sleep.

She went with him for therapy treatments, and encouraged him through the painful process of exercising his injured hip. He was pale and exhausted when they returned to the room, and she stood by his bed, alternately holding his hand and wiping perspiration from his face as he tried to relax his throbbing, aching muscles.

"I've never had to lie in bed before," he murmured, after a particularly painful therapy session. "That's worse than the pain."

"I know, but you're doing better each day."

"I feel weak as a baby. How long will it take me to get well?"

"The doctor hasn't said. Don't fret about it."

"But I'm so weak, I can't even hold you in my arms. I want to kiss you, Norah, and I'm not even strong enough to do that. But is there any reason why you can't kiss me?"

With a smile, and hoping a nurse wouldn't come in, Norah's open lips slowly lowered to his, and she kissed him with a hunger that contradicted her outward composure.

When her lips raised from his with a gentle caress, Mason stared at her wonderingly. Even in his weakened condition, he was shocked at his eager response to the touch of her lips. He opened his mouth to say, "I love you, Norah," then he remembered his wounds.

Since Norah had turned down the proposal from Louis Masters, was she his for the taking? But thoughts of his condition sealed Mason's lips. If he couldn't recover his former vitality, he wouldn't bind Norah to an invalid husband. After spending her youth caring for her brother, she deserved something better than that.

Each morning when Norah came, she kissed Mason, and repeated the gesture when she left for the night. Although Norah knew he looked forward to her caresses, she couldn't imagine why he didn't respond to her kiss as he'd done the first day.

Paul and Mary made it a point to be at the hospital when the doctor discussed Mason's release. Norah was relieved to have them with her, for if the news wasn't good, she didn't want to be alone with Mason when he learned the doctor's prognosis.

The doctor sat on the edge of Mason's bed. ''You're more fortunate than seems possible, given the severity of that accident,'' he said, ''and you can expect a full recovery, but it will take time.''

''Thank God,'' Paul said.

The surgeon nodded. ''Yes, surgeons always need His help. We've repaired your broken hip, Mason, and if you'll do what I tell you to, it will heal completely. Only time can heal the broken ribs and bruises. As I understand, you live alone. If you can't arrange for someone to stay with you for a few weeks, I want you to stay in our rehab center. That might be a good idea anyway. If you go home, you may take it into your head to start working. And I don't want you riding a horse or driving a tractor for at least two months, maybe longer, depending on how quickly you heal.''

''That's pretty tough medicine for a rancher, Doc,'' Mason said slowly.

''I realize that, but a crippled rancher isn't much good, either, so you'll have to choose between inactivity for a few months or limping in pain the rest of your life.''

''That isn't much choice,'' Mason replied grimly.

''Exactly! So this is what I recommend. If you do go home, you must come to the hospital three days a week for therapy. If you stay on the walker, and do what I tell you, you should mend quickly. So, what'll it be? Do you have anyone who can stay with you for at least a month, or will you remain here?''

''I happen to be out of a job right now, Mason,'' Norah said, her lips twitching with a smile. ''If you want me to, I'll come to the Flying K and be your nurse. I'm experienced in nursing, as you know. Doug and Paul will be busy with the ranch work, and I can drive you back and forth for the therapy sessions, too.''

Mason's eyes brightened, but he protested, ''I'd

like that, but I don't want to interfere with your other plans.''

Norah had spoken impetuously, and she wondered if she should have volunteered. ''I don't actually have any plans right now, so it'll work out all right.''

Mason's roommate left the day before Mason was released from the hospital, and as they were alone in the room, Norah took the opportunity to tell Mason about her weekend at Mahoney State Park and how she'd made her decision not to marry Louis. She'd been wondering how she could tell him what he wanted to know without putting him under any obligation. By staying in Broken Bow to be with Mason, she'd obviously betrayed her feelings to the Johnsons, but had Mason detected that she loved him?

So she told him about her experience with Miss Emma, of how she'd wasted a lot of her life fretting because she couldn't go to the mission field, not appreciating the opportunities of serving at home.

''No matter where your interest was, you did stay at home, so don't be so hard on yourself.''

''But it's humbling to know that I couldn't see that God wanted me where I was. I've wasted a lot of time hoping for that which apparently can't be. But because of my interest in world missions, I've contributed a great deal of what money I had to send other people, who might have been more qualified than I. Fortunately, God hasn't given up on me yet.''

''I've had a lot of rough years, too,'' Mason said, ''but through my difficulties, there is one thing I've never doubted. God is true to His promises, but He expects us to believe He'll do what He says He will.''

''That's a wonderful concept, Mason—one I wish I'd learned a long time ago.''

''So what do you think God wants you to do now?'' Mason asked hesitantly, not meeting Norah's gaze.

''I'm not sure. The answer is just around the bend, and I'll know when I get to it. For the present, I believe God wants me to provide the help you need. When you're able to get along without me, I'll take the next step.''

Judging from the serious expression in Mason's eyes, Norah wasn't surprised that his words echoed her own thoughts. ''I don't think I'll ever be able to get along without you.''

Now that they knew Mason would soon be released from the hospital, Sheila and Norah took two days to winterize the Bar 8 ranch house, and Norah moved her possessions to the Flying K ranch. They also had a hospital bed delivered, because it would be easier for him to get in and out of a bed that could be adjusted more conveniently than an ordinary bed. The doctor still wanted Mason to have a lot of bed rest.

Norah stayed at the Flying K alone the night before Mason's release. She knew this was the last time for weeks that she'd have an introspective time without Mason's disturbing presence. If Mason did love her, she sensed he wouldn't say anything until she definitely made up her mind that she no longer intended to pursue an overseas mission ministry.

At this point, she was willing to give up that dream, but it would be difficult to say goodbye to her desire to be a missionary until God showed her what He wanted her to do. But in her newfound faith, she had to move forward and not look back. Was it a lack of faith to wonder what God had ahead for her? Or to question what would fill the empty vacuum in her heart where she'd nurtured a dream for more than twenty years?

Should she tell Mason she'd given up going to the mission field and see what his reaction would be? Just thinking about her lost dream depressed her. How would she feel if she actually put it into words?

But then a thought hit Norah like a bolt out of the blue. If God had really wanted her to go to the mission field, He would have created such a strong desire to go that *nothing* would have stopped her from going—not her father's request nor her brother's ill health. If her calling had been to Africa or some other overseas area, God would have provided the way for her to go, as well as guiding her father to make some other provision for a housekeeper.

Suddenly her mind was free from the guilty feeling she'd harbored for so long. It pained her to think of the many hours she'd wasted fretting about something that wasn't to be. Wondering if the Bible had any parallels to her situation, she remembered that the Apostle Paul had once been prevented from going to a place he wanted to go. She opened her Bible to the book of Acts and found the incident. Paul and his companions "had been kept by the Holy Spirit from preaching the word in the province of Asia." And when they'd tried to enter Bithynia, the Bible said, "but the Spirit of Jesus would not allow them to."

As she read the account, she sensed the disappointment Paul must have felt, his frustration that he couldn't go where he wanted to preach the Gospel. She could identify with his dashed hopes, his desire to serve the Lord, only to find a roadblock in his way. Why didn't God want Paul to continue his missionary work in Asia Minor? Had Paul asked that same question? Had he gone to bed with a troubled mind, a forlorn hope that his service to God might not be needed anymore?

But during that night, Paul had a vision of a man

begging the apostle to come to Macedonia to help his people. Paul had his answer. There were other missionaries working in Asia Minor, but God had a special purpose for Paul in Europe. And what a special purpose that was! For when Paul crossed the Aegean Sea into Europe, he became the forerunner of those who brought the Gospel to Europe and ultimately to America. Norah could imagine that Paul set forward on that journey with confidence and new strength, secure in the knowledge that He was doing God's will.

Norah didn't expect a vision, because now people had the Bible and the Holy Spirit to guide them in making decisions. But as she sat in Mason's big chair and felt the comforting warmth of his presence, once and for all, she accepted that the call to service when she was a girl had *not* been to overseas missions. As she prepared for bed, she wondered if, like Paul, before morning she would have a vision of where else God was leading her.

Morning didn't bring an answer to her long-range future, but as she waited for Paul Johnson to go with her to get Mason, she definitely knew that God, at this moment wanted her to be of service to Mason. She repeated Miss Emma's slogan, ''God knows best what is best for me.''

''My car is small, but I don't think he should try getting in a truck,'' Norah said to Paul when they were trying to decide which vehicle to take. "Let's take mine this morning, and see if it's large enough for him. If so, I can manage to take him for therapy treatments."

"Are you nervous about what you've agreed to do?" Paul said as they left the Flying K.

"After taking care of my sick father and an invalid brother, the physical part isn't going to be difficult. But I have had second thoughts about whether I should have volunteered to do this. I don't want Mason, or any of the neighbors, to get the wrong idea. Surely there won't be any gossip about us."

"If you believe this is the right thing for you to do, I wouldn't worry about what other people might think. You'll be a godsend to Mason. However, you won't have an easy time. Mason has never been sick, and I doubt he'll be a cooperative patient. You'll have your hands full trying to get him to do what the doctor says."

"You're probably right, but I think his common sense will prevail, and he'll realize that it's either stay inside now or maybe the rest of his life."

"That's true, but he's not used to staying indoors, and he's going to be cranky. I just hope you don't get on each other's nerves so much that you'll pack up and leave the Sand Hills. Given half a chance, I think you and Mason might be the answer to each other's problems.''

''If he's any crankier than my father, he'll be really bad. I'm not going to make any rash promises, but I think I'll be able to handle his bad moments.''

Mason was sitting in a wheelchair when they reached his room, and the expression on his face wasn't promising.

''I've been using a walker to navigate around, and I don't see any reason why I can't go to the car on my own two feet,'' he said with an indignant stare at the determined nurse standing beside him.

''It does appear that way,'' Norah said soothingly, ''but let's try the nurse's way first. He's had more experience with your type of injury then we have. Besides, it's hospital policy. The main thing all of us want, including the hospital staff, is for you to have a full recovery.''

A bit shamefacedly, Mason said, ''I guess you're right,'' and Paul Johnson gave Norah a thumbs-up behind Mason's back.

Norah received Mason's therapy schedule and instructions for his home care. As two members of the hospital staff moved Mason from the wheelchair to the car, a look of pain crossed his face. He remained silent while they drove away from the hospital, through the business section of town, and started north on Route 2.

"I guess I'm not as agile as I thought I was," Mason admitted. "My hip doesn't bother me as much as the rest of my body. Whenever I take a deep breath, I feel like someone's stuck a knife in my ribs."

"Then you won't mind lying in bed for most of another month?" Paul asked.

"I didn't say I wouldn't mind," Mason growled, "but I can see why I have to."

Doug and Sheila were at the Flying K when they arrived, and Doug had just finished building a ramp to the front door of the ranch house.

"Drive down by the outbuildings," Mason told Paul. "I have a feeling I'm not going to be out of the house until I go for my first therapy session, and I want to see what happened."

"We haven't done anything more with the cleanup effort," Paul said. "When you give the word, we'll get rid of that debris."

"No hurry," Mason said. "I don't have the money now to build the kind of barn I want to. I'll have to give it some thought. At least thinking won't hurt my leg."

Pete and Repeat barked their welcome and Doug had to restrain them from jumping on Mason and causing him to lose his balance. Mason did stoop and rub their heads, and that seemed to satisfy them.

Mason approved of the change they'd made in his

house by placing the hospital bed in front of the living room window—a position that looked out over the ranch buildings, but also allowed him to watch television if he wanted. And the trip from the hospital had been so wearing on his strength, he was ready to lie down. Over Mason's protests, Doug and Paul helped him into the bed.

"One of us will come every morning to help you take a shower and do the ranch chores," Paul said.

"They taught me in therapy how to manage my personal habits," Mason protested. "Go on with your work. Norah and I'll manage all right."

"The hospital bathrooms are better equipped for walkers and wheelchairs," Paul continued, ignoring Mason's protests. "We've added some rails in the bathroom, but we'll still come to help you until I'm satisfied you're strong enough to manage." Turning to Norah, Paul said, "And if you need us anytime, night or day, you can reach one of us by phone. We'll be here in no time."

Norah smiled her thanks as the Johnsons left her and Mason alone. She stood beside his bed as they watched his friends drive away. Mason reached for her hand and lifted it to his face.

"I shouldn't have let you do this, Norah. You've spent enough of your life waiting on invalids. You need someone to take care of you now."

"I've thought that I probably shouldn't have volunteered to stay with you—guess I pushed my company on you. But we're stuck with each other, right or wrong.''

''If I have to have a nurse, there's no one else on earth I'd rather have than you!''

''I want to stay, and you want me here, so we're both satisfied. It's time for some medicine. Why don't you take it and rest a while?''

He nodded agreement. ''Seeing the pile of rubble that fell on me makes me wonder why God chose to spare me at this particular time. Apparently there's still work He wants me to do here on earth. The past couple of weeks when the pain was unbearable, I wished I had gone to Heaven.''

The comment alerted Norah to how much his death would have devastated her. To have lost Mason before he ever belonged to her would have shattered her.

''It's customary at the Flying K to never sell our old horses or put them down. When a horse gets too old to work, we turn him out to pasture and look after him until he dies. We usually have a pasture full of old crocks lazying around, waiting to die. I was beginning to think that's where I'd end up.''

''Don't even have such thoughts,'' Norah scolded, and whacked him lightly on the shoulder. ''We'll soon have you back in the saddle again.''

''I know. I've made enough improvement in the

past week to believe that even an old crock like me must still have some living to do.''

"Of course you have. We can't judge our lives by the number of years, but by what we accomplish along the way. Is there anything special you want for supper?''

"I haven't had much of an appetite, but I figure that's going to change when I start eating your food. Fix what you want—I'll like it.''

Chapter Sixteen

While Mason slept, Norah brought her basket and sat in a rocker near his bed. She was behind with the crocheted shawls and bed jackets she'd been making for nursing homes in Springfield, a separate project. Her goal was fifty each year, and considering the hours she'd spent with H & H this summer, she hadn't had much time for needlework.

Mason was watching her before she realized he was awake. When she became aware that his eyes were on her, she put her crocheting in the basket. "Why didn't you tell me you were awake? I didn't want to make any noise to disturb you, so I've been waiting to prepare supper."

"Do you know how wonderful it is to see you sitting there? I'm inclined to believe the old adage that it takes a woman to make a home.'' He looked around the room where Norah had placed several of the personal items she'd brought from the Bar 8. ''This room has never seemed so homey.''

''I have a casserole prepared, and I'll pop that in the microwave. Supper will be ready soon. I'll bring a pan of water for you to wash up.''

''No, I'm going to the bathroom. I'm supposed to walk several times a day. Then I'll sit in a chair for supper.''

She put the casserole in the oven. ''I'll walk behind you in case you need help.''

It hurt Norah to see Mason limping along like an old man, but she was comforted to know that it was only temporary. ''Paul took the door off the bathroom so you can maneuver the walker easier.''

''Hey! That doesn't give much privacy.''

''It will be all right,'' she said as she left him at the door of the bathroom. ''Please call when you're ready to start back. We don't need any heroics around here. You have to be careful until your hip heals.''

After supper, Norah perched on the foot of his bed and placed a wide cutting board between them. ''Let's play Scrabble.'' She scattered the small letter blocks on the board. ''I brought this box from the Bar 8. You probably know how to play. We each draw several letters and make words with them.''

Mason entered into the game enthusiastically, at first, but when he started yawning, she knew his medication was taking effect.

"Lights out!" she said.

"I guess so," Mason agreed, "but I'll be glad when I can stop taking this pain medicine. It gives me bad dreams."

"Call me if you need anything. I'll keep the bedroom door open."

She turned out the lights, leaving only a dim lamp burning near his bed. When she bent over him, Mason's large fingers wrapped gently around her chin, and his breath fanned her face. Her heart raced when his lips pressed against hers, leaving her mouth soft and warm. With a contented sigh, she buried her face in the hollow between his shoulder and neck. She brushed a gentle kiss on his neck and drew away from his warm embrace.

"Good night," she whispered.

Dealing with the emotions Mason's kiss had stirred in her heart kept Norah awake, and she hadn't been asleep very long when she was awakened by his muttering. He might be talking in his sleep, but she hurried down the hallway. Mason was writhing on the bed, as if he were in pain.

She laid a light hand on his shoulder, and he quieted. "Mason, are you all right?"

"Norah?"

"Yes, I'm here. Are you hurting?"

"All over," he said.

"I'll massage your leg muscles, and after that, why don't you sit in a chair, so I can work on your shoulders?"

Her skilled fingers soon brought ease to his aches, and he said, "You're good at this, Norah—much better than the nurses at the hospital. You should have been a nurse."

Norah laughed at his comment as she applied lotion to his back and shoulders. "I may be confused about what God's calling was, but I'm sure he never intended me to be a nurse. I can only perform these functions for people I—" She stopped short of saying, "people I love," and stammered, "people I know."

She gave his back a final pat and drew his shirt into place.

"How about some hot tea?" she asked. "I have decaf, so it won't keep you awake."

And to Norah it didn't seem at all unusual that, at two o'clock in the morning, they sat together drinking tea.

Their days and nights developed a similar pattern. For the first two weeks, the long trips into Broken Bow for therapy kept Mason so weak and irritable that he wasn't sure he would ever return to normal health. But each time, the therapist assured Mason he was making progress. When the doctor relaxed some of the restrictions he'd placed on Mason, Paul started taking Mason on short trips in the truck to look over the ranch.

Since the driveway to the mailbox was black-topped, with Mason riding in his wheelchair, Norah took him to pick up the mail each day. He was with her when she received a letter from her Realtor.

"I'm going to open this now," she said excitedly. "I hope he's sold the house. Do you want me to read it aloud?"

"Yes, please."

"Dear Norah,

"I have some terrific news for you. A development company is buying property in Springfield to build a shopping mall, and they've chosen several blocks of land where your house is located. That's the good news. Now the bad news is that the house will be razed. I know it will hurt to have your birthplace demolished, but before you get too grieved over that, consider that they're offering $500,000 for the property. That's much more than you can hope to get if it's sold for a residence. Let me know as soon as possible if you'll take the offer."

"That's more than what I'm asking for the Bar 8."

But Norah hardly heard him. If she was still dreaming about going to the mission field, this amount would more than pay for her expenses. But wisely invested, it would also provide her with some old-age security. Since she'd never had a job outside the home, she didn't have the retirement benefits many people did.

Thoughtfully pushing Mason back to the house, she remembered what he'd said about the Bar 8. "Then I hope you're as successful in selling as I've been."

"Does it bother you to have your family home destroyed?"

"Yes, it does. My grandfather Williamson built the house. It was a wonderful building once, but it's an *old* house now. I'll call the Realtor right away."

"Then you're going to accept the offer?"

"Don't you think I should?"

"I don't have any idea about real estate prices in Missouri, but the Realtor seems to think it's a good offer."

"He's been a friend of our family for years, so I can rely on his judgment."

Norah telephoned the Realtor before she and Mason left for his therapy treatment. The assurance that there was little doubt that the developer would be able to buy all the land he needed contributed to her mounting excitement throughout the day.

Mason was happy for her windfall, but he wondered what difference the sale of her property would make between them. The doctor kept assuring him that he was making progress, but Mason still wasn't sure he would be physically able to run the Flying K as he had before. He couldn't speak to her about a future until he was well again.

And Norah tried to suppress her excitement, because until she saw which door God chose to open for her, she couldn't talk with Mason about the future. Before she went to sleep that night, she thanked God for His faithfulness, and for the sale of her home. She asked for His continued guidance and closed her prayer with the assurance she'd learned from Miss Emma. "God knows best what is best for me."

Norah didn't believe modern-day visions were necessary, but when she awakened the next morning, she had no doubts about what she should do.

"My, you look chipper this morning," Mason said crankily when she entered the living room, a broad smile on her face and peace in her heart.

He groaned when he sat up and tried to get out of bed. She rushed to his side. "Didn't you sleep well?"

"Oh, don't pay any attention to me. I'm always

tired after a therapy session.'' He knew that mental stress was partially to blame for keeping him awake. He was getting better, and it wouldn't be long until he didn't need a nurse. Once he was able to stay alone, Norah would leave.

He was strong enough now that he could walk without Norah's assistance, so while he took a shower and dressed for the day, Norah made a telephone call.

Speaking quietly, she said, ''Paul, you mentioned you were going to a cattle sale today—do you think Mason is up to going?''

''What does Mason think about it?''

She laughed nervously. ''He's taking a shower now, and I don't want him to know I telephoned you. I have some things to do that I don't want him to know about. It would be helpful if you'd keep him occupied today.''

''Sure, Norah, I'll take care of him,'' Paul said. ''I can take a folding chair so he'll have a comfortable place to sit. This will be good for him—I should have thought about it myself. I'll telephone and arrange it.''

Feeling a little ashamed because she was deceiving him, Norah prepared Mason's favorite breakfast—buckwheat cakes, maple syrup and sausage.

The shower must have loosened his joints, because when he came into the kitchen, a satisfied expression on his face, he was walking unassisted.

"Mason! Where's your walker?"

"I don't need it in the house."

She hurried down the hall and came back with the walker, which she deliberately placed beside his chair.

"Please, Mason, you've been so good. It's only a few more weeks—don't get reckless now."

"I'm tired of being an invalid," he complained.

She brushed back his hair that was still damp from the shower and kissed the soft spot behind his ear. Kneeling beside his chair, she placed her arms around his waist carefully for his ribs were still tender to the touch.

"I understand that. And I want you back to normal as much as you want it, so please don't do anything to overset the recovery you've made."

Shamefaced, Mason leaned his head on hers. "I'm sorry, my dear, I didn't mean to upset you. I thought you'd be pleased to see I could walk alone."

"And I am, but don't rush it."

"Forgive me for upsetting you. Now that I'm getting stronger, it's hard to stay idle. There's so much to do on the ranch—things I won't ask Paul and Doug to do. I must have a barn built before winter sets in, and I'll have to borrow money to build the kind of barn I need. I can't do a thing about it until I'm on my feet again.''

"It will all work out. The first thing is to concentrate on a full recovery.''

She started to stand, but Mason held her in place proving that he had indeed gained a lot of strength.

"Have I told you how much you've meant to me in the past few weeks? I don't know how you've been so patient. I love you, Norah, and I believe you love me, but I'm not going to say anything more until the doctor gives me a clean bill of health. You've spent most of your life taking care of your brother and father—I won't ask you to do the same for me. It's time you had someone to look after you.''

The ringing telephone interrupted them, and Norah brought Mason the cordless phone. Norah knew it was Paul Johnson when Mason said, "I'd sure like to go, Paul. I'm getting cabin fever, but let me see what Norah thinks about it.''

He turned to Norah, whose face flushed guiltily, and she found it difficult to meet his glance.

"Paul wants to take me to an auction today. Do you think I should?''

"I'm sure he'll take good care of you. The weather forecaster predicted a summerlike day, so why not?''

Mason thanked Paul, saying he'd be ready when Paul came by in an hour.

"But what will you do all day?" Mason questioned. "I hate to leave you alone."

"I have some shopping and banking to do, so I'll drive into Valentine this morning."

Even though Norah did feel guilty for prodding Paul into inviting Mason, his enthusiasm for being out with his fellow ranchers again made Norah happy for him. She'd forced herself not to smother him with her attentions, but he'd come to the place where he readily asked for help in things he couldn't do. Pulling on his boots, for instance, was a chore that took both of their skills, and they were usually panting and laughing at the end of each attempt.

But when Paul stopped his car in front of the house, Mason was ready except for his wide-brimmed hat, which Norah perched on his head at a rakish angle.

"I'm going to miss you, Norah. Doesn't seem possible that we've been constant companions for over a month and haven't gotten on each other's nerves. At least, you haven't gotten on mine."

"I've enjoyed being here."

"Got a kiss for me before I leave?" With his right hand on the table, he steadied himself and put his left arm around her midriff. Norah relaxed into his embrace, enjoying the feel of his hand on her waist.

His kiss was slow and tender with a promise of more to come.

Their intimate caress was broken by Paul's booming voice. "Are you going to an auction or staying here to kiss your nurse?"

Mason slowly lifted his lips, his eyes searching Norah's, and he said to Paul, "I do find her company more appealing than yours, but I'll try to make it through the day with you."

Paul held Mason's arm as he negotiated the one step to the ground-level porch. Norah knew that Paul would take good care of him, so she hurried with her shower and dressing. Before she left for Valentine, she telephoned the Realtor in Springfield and received good news.

"The deal is going through," he said, "and I got twenty thousand more than originally offered. Your lot is a large one, and very important to the location of the development. In fact, the way the land lies close to the river, if they couldn't buy your property, the developer might have backed out of the deal. The papers will be ready to sign within the month. Will you be home by then, or shall I mail them to you?"

"I'm not sure. If I leave here, I'll contact you. Otherwise, just mail them to the address you've used all summer."

Chapter Seventeen

Norah returned from Valentine a half hour before Paul and Mason got back to the Flying K. The answering machine light was blinking, but having a good idea what the message was, she waited for Mason to receive it. She changed into blue jeans and a sweatshirt, and was starting supper when saw them turn off the highway onto the Flying K road. She waited for Mason on the porch. Lines of fatigue etched his face, but his eyes gleamed with pleasure.

"I got along all right today," he said when he reached Norah. "For the first time I'm hopeful that I'll make a full recovery."

"Of course you'll make a full recovery. I've never doubted that."

"But I *am* tired," he said. "Do I have time for a nap before supper?"

"Yes. I don't have the food ready yet."

She waved to Paul, who was heading toward the stable. "I'll check on things before I go."

"Want to eat supper with us?"

"No, thanks. Mary will be looking for me."

"Thanks a lot," Norah said.

Norah didn't call attention to the blinking light on the answering machine, for she thought Mason needed rest. He slept for an hour, breathing deeply, and when she thought he'd had sufficient rest, but not too much to ruin his night's sleep, she started rattling the kitchen utensils. He roused, swung his feet off the bed, yawning and threading his fingers through his hair.

"I've been dead to the world." When he saw the time, he said, "You should have called me."

As he started toward the bathroom, he said, "We apparently have a message," and he pushed the play button on the answering machine.

Norah's hands tightened on the edge of the sink where she was preparing salad.

"Hey, Mason," the voice of the Valentine Realtor sounded in the room. "I have a buyer for the Bar 8. I took a two months' option today for the sale of the property. Give me a call if you're home before five o'clock, and we can talk over details."

"At last!" Mason said joyfully. "I wondered if I'd ever sell the place. It's too late to telephone him tonight, but I'll sleep better knowing I'm out of the woods financially.''

''But what happens to Sheila and Doug when you've sold the ranch?'' Norah asked, for she'd been concerned about them.

''Doug is buying a ranch that adjoins Paul's. I've helped him by furnishing a house and hiring him to keep an eye on the Bar 8. He's been saving all the money I've paid him so he can build a house on their property. They'll be okay.''

Norah dallied with the cleaning-up chores as long as she could, but finally she went to her bedroom and came back with an envelope. She waited quietly until the newscast Mason was watching had finished, before she said, ''Mason, we need to have a serious talk.''

He clicked the off button on the remote. Turning to face her, he said, ''You're not planning to leave!''

Smiling slightly, she said, ''No, I'm not. I'm buying the Bar 8.''

He stared at her, speechless. When he did speak, he said angrily, ''I won't sell it to you. It's a poor investment. I won't let you sink money in a ranch that I can't even make a profit on. It's out of the question.''

''But, Mason, I awakened this morning with the overwhelming conviction that God is nudging me in that direction. I'll buy the ranch and lease it to the

H & H year-round. The amount Jim Hanson said they would pay seems like a good return on my investment. Besides, don't you see? This *is* my missionary work—to provide therapy for those who are mentally and physically impaired.''

He shook his head emphatically. ''No, Norah, I won't have it! I know why you're doing this. And I won't have you risk your inheritance to solve my financial problems.''

''Didn't you listen to what I said? This will be my missionary work, serving in the way God can use me.''

''And you'd be staying in the Sand Hills.''

''Yes.''

''You've never spent a winter up here. You might not like it.''

Norah was hurt that he was finding fault with her plan. She'd thought he would be overjoyed that she'd found her mission field in the Sand Hills.

''I thought you'd be pleased to have me for your neighbor.''

''I don't want you for a neighbor. I want you for my wife.'' His anger surprised the words right out of his mouth. ''And I don't want to be under obligation to my wife for saving me financially. I'd feel as if I was marrying you for your money.''

''You can't keep me from buying the Bar 8,'' Norah said stubbornly. ''This is a business deal and has nothing to do with marriage. If that's a proposal, it sure is a poor one, and I won't demean myself by replying to it.''

Norah ran down the hallway into her bedroom and slammed the door—the first time the door had been closed since he'd come home from the hospital. Norah wasn't normally a weepy woman, but she lay facedown on the bed and reached for a tissue to blow her nose and wipe her eyes.

When she'd left the bedroom this morning, she'd been convinced that this was the answer to her relationship with Mason. Her dream of a mission field would be realized, while at the same time, she and Mason could be together. He said he wanted her to be his wife, but why would he expect her to give up the divine calling she'd nurtured all of these years? He'd seemed so happy the past few weeks when she'd been at his instant beck and call. As his wife, would Mason resent her involvement in the H & H program?

Norah's reaction to his refusal stunned Mason. He was only trying to protect her investment. Obviously she didn't have the foggiest idea about running a ranch, or any kind of business for that matter. Her family involvement had sheltered Norah from the work-a-day world, and what kind of a man would he be if he took advantage of her inexperience and sold the Bar 8 to her? Would she buy the ranch if he didn't own it, if she didn't know he needed to sell that ranch to hang on to the Flying K? He had a sneaky suspicion that she wouldn't, and if she lost her money, he didn't want that on his conscience.

But he did feel low to have hurt her when she wanted to help him. He limped down the hallway, but when he was confronted with the closed door, he returned to the living room. They could work out the situation tomorrow.

Norah heard Mason's steps at the door, and she was tempted to go to him, but she knew she couldn't talk to him without crying, so she changed into her nightclothes and went to bed. Ashamed of her behavior, she didn't look forward to facing him in the morning.

An awkward silence stretched between them when Mason sat at the table for his breakfast. Norah placed his plate before him and sat beside him with only a cup of coffee. Feeling like a hypocrite, he prayed for God's blessing on the food, but he was dumbstruck. Although he and Norah had never had any difficulty conversing before, he couldn't think of anything to say, and she didn't seem inclined to talk. He ate the oatmeal and toast in silence while she occasionally sipped her coffee. Her eyes were downcast.

Clearing his throat, Mason said, "I didn't mean to make you mad."

"I'm not mad. You have your opinion and I have mine." Standing, she said, "Do you want anything else to eat or drink?"

"No."

"We must leave for your therapy session in an hour," she reminded Mason.

He telephoned the Realtor, in Norah's hearing, saying, "I heard your message about the option, but I'm not sure I'll go through with the sale. Put a hold on that option until I'm in touch."

Mason listened to the Realtor's remarks.

"Perhaps I am being foolish, but there are other matters I'm considering right now. I'll contact you in a few days."

Try as she might, on the trip to the hospital, Norah couldn't think of anything to say, and the ride was made mostly in silence. Always before, the time had passed quickly, but with a silent Mason beside her, Norah was miserable. Even though they hadn't talked constantly during their time together, she'd never sensed the restraint that bound their lips now.

They couldn't even rejoice together over the doctor's report that Mason wouldn't require any further therapy at the hospital. The therapist gave instructions for exercises that he should continue to do at home, and with a sinking feeling, Mason realized he wouldn't need a nurse any longer.

"I want to see you again in two months, and at that time," the surgeon instructed, "I'll expect you to walk into my office without a limp. Continue your work now, but at a slower pace. Start out working a few hours a day, driving short distances at first, and by the end of those months, you should be back on your normal schedule."

"I'm really pleased for you, Mason," Norah said as they left the hospital. "You've been a good patient."

He shook his head. "Not very. I had a good nurse."

Tears misted her eyes, but Norah said, "Do you want to drive part of the way home?"

"I'd like that. I may have forgotten how to drive."

She handed him the key. "Be sure and tell me if you have any pain."

"I'll drive about half the way. I've suffered enough already—I'm not going to jeopardize my recovery now."

The ice had been broken by these exchanges, and they talked sporadically as they traveled, but only about the scenery and the many migratory birds they saw. They didn't mention the things that mattered most because their easy camaraderie was gone, and

Norah mourned the passing of that as if she'd lost a loved one.

During supper, Norah turned the television on so they could watch the evening news, and that made the time more bearable. After they ate, Mason walked around the room several times, and the way he eased down in his chair, Norah could tell the long ride had been difficult for him.

She was preparing the coffeemaker for breakfast when the phone rang. The majority of the calls were for Mason, so Norah was surprised when he said, "Just a minute," and held the phone toward her.

Norah walked to him and took the phone. "Sheila?"

"No. A man."

"Norah." Her brother Sam's voice sounded in her ear, and Norah sat quickly in the chair beside Mason.

Lifting her eyebrows in Mason's direction, Norah said, "Hello, Sam—good to hear from you," wondering if it was good. It was the first time she'd talked to Sam since he'd accused her of being "a foolish old maid." She mouthed, "My brother," to Mason, and pushed the speaker phone button so he could hear the conversation.

"I thought you intended to come home at the end of summer. It's almost November, and you still aren't here."

"The therapy program has ended, but I have another job now. I'm taking care of a rancher who's been involved in an accident. I don't know when I'll return to Missouri, if I ever do."

"I hear you've sold our home."

"I've agreed to, if the deal goes through as planned."

"Oh, it will. The new development is the greatest topic of conversation in Springfield these days. There's no doubt about it. How much money did you get for the house?"

"Sorry, Sam, but that's confidential information."

"I've heard rumors that you're getting lots of money. Are you going to divide with the rest of us?"

"Why, no, I hadn't considered it! The rest of you got Father's money—the house is my only inheritance."

"But we didn't get as much as you'll receive from the sale of the house. I think you owe us."

Recriminations rushed to Norah's lips, but she brushed them aside. "It may seem a bit uneven, but don't forget that Father paid for college for you and the girls. The cost of four years of higher education for each of you was quite expensive."

"What are you going to do with the money?"

"I've taken an option on a piece of property,"

Norah said evenly, and changed the subject. "How are our sisters getting along?"

"All right, I guess. I haven't seen them for several days. Norah, this isn't the last you've heard about that money." And without saying goodbye, he hung up the phone.

With a trembling voice, Norah said, "You've asked me several times why I haven't contacted my family. Now do you understand why?"

"Yes. How can they be so different from you?"

She shook her head. "I'm afraid I haven't been very good company today, Mason. I'm going to bed."

He let her go, for what could he say to ease the pain he knew she must feel over this kind of treatment from the siblings she'd served for most of her adult life? And he knew his attitude about the Bar 8 hadn't helped her situation. Maybe it *was* God's will for Nora to own the ranch and provide a haven for the therapy program. If so, where did that leave their relationship?

As he thought of the situation, it seemed the perfect solution to both their problems. She needed a mission field. He needed a barn. He wanted to marry her, but had feared she might not want to remain in the Sand Hills. She'd made the decision to stay here independently of marriage to him, so he wouldn't have to wonder if she'd ever blame him for asking her to stay.

So why had he reacted so negatively? Because he didn't like the idea of his wife being independent? Even though he loved Norah, did he still think he should marry a younger woman who could give him an heir for the Flying K? He knew women today, well into their forties, gave birth without any problems. But would the idea appeal to Norah? He'd made an idol out of his ranch—putting it before his own happiness. He was convinced he could be happy living anywhere with Norah at his side, so didn't that prove that an heir was no longer important to him? When he got too old to operate the ranch, he could sell it to Doug, who was like a son to him anyway. Should he go to Norah now and let her know? He was sure she wasn't sleeping, for she hadn't closed her door tonight, and he could often hear her turning in bed. But he stayed in the living room.

The walls of the old ranch house seemed to vibrate all night with unspoken thoughts as both Mason and Norah fought their own personal battles and concerns for the future.

For the first time since Norah had become estranged from her family, she came to grips with the bitterness she'd harbored in her heart against her siblings. She placed her unforgiving spirit before God, also realizing that there was some bitterness against her father for expecting her to take over the household duties as she had. But each time when she asked God's forgiveness, she found no peace of heart and mind. Instead, over and over in her mind, she thought of Jesus's words in the eleventh chapter of Mark. "And when you stand praying, if you hold anything against anyone, forgive him, so that your Father in heaven may forgive you your sins."

Sleep didn't come for Norah until she realized what she should do and agreed in her heart that she would do it without delay. She awakened early, sat in a chair by the bedside table and started a letter she should have written long ago.

She had just finished the message when Mason walked down the hallway and stopped at her open door.

"Is it all right if I come in?"

"Sure," she said, smiling brightly at him. He wondered at her change of attitude as he sat on the foot of her bed. He hardly knew how to start, but he noticed the paper she held.

"Been writing a letter or your memoirs?" he quizzed lightly.

"A letter." She handed him the single sheet of paper. "Read it, and see if it's okay."

He gave her a sidelong glance of surprise as he took the letter and read it aloud.

"Dear Sam,

"Our conversation last night caused me a great deal of distress. It hasn't been easy for me to be at odds with my family, for I love all of you. I don't feel that I've done anything to cause your animosity toward me, however, I've spent a restless night remembering the words of Jesus. 'When you stand praying, if you hold anything against anyone, forgive him, so that your Father in heaven may forgive you your sins.'

"So I want you to know that I have forgiven you for your thoughtless disregard of my personal needs. I forgive you for not appreciating the years I spent helping our family.

"This doesn't mean that I'll give you any of the money I receive from the sale of the house. I won't buy your affection. Besides, I've already made plans to invest the money.

"Please share this message with our sisters. Whether or not you want to accept my forgiveness in a manner that will allow us to continue as a family will be up to you. Now that I've forgiven you and asked God to forgive me, I'm at peace with myself and God. Regardless of your decision, I'll never stop praying for you.

Your sister, Norah.''

When Mason lifted his head, he looked at Norah with a definite realization that he must not lose this woman. He wanted to share the rest of her life. They'd reached the point where their relationship must be resolved. He moved closer to her, taking her hand that still held the pen she'd used to write the forgiving note to her brother. He softly removed the pen and kissed her palm.

''I want to ask your forgiveness, too,'' he said. ''I've not been very understanding the past couple of days. I suppose my ego has been hurting because I thought you were buying the Bar 8 to help me. But if you're convinced that this is the way God wants you to go, I won't oppose you anymore.''

''I have no doubts, and I *am* going to buy the Bar 8,'' she said, her chin lifting in determination, with a challenge in her eyes.

Laughing, he threw up his hands. ''I give up! I'm not going to battle you about it.''

''Good,'' she said.

''Since you've made the decision to buy the ranch, that means you like the country and are willing to stay here.''

''Right.''

''Then will you stay as my wife?''

Her eyelashes fluttered on her cheeks, and she wouldn't meet his gaze.

"I've wanted to marry you since the first night you came to the Flying K," Mason continued. "But I've thought up all kinds of reasons why I shouldn't ask you."

When he paused, Norah prompted, "Such as?"

"I had no right to ask you to marry me and give up your dream of missionary work. Besides, my wife had died in childbirth, so I wouldn't risk another woman's life in that way. The more I loved you, the more reasons popped up that kept us apart."

Norah held up her hand. "Mason, we don't live in the Dark Ages anymore. Women a lot older than I am have healthy children every day. Besides, my own mother was forty-five when Sam was born."

His eyes lightened. "Is that a fact! Then you wouldn't be afraid to have children?"

"Of course not."

The eagerness faded from his eyes. "You might not be too old to be a mother at forty-two, but I sure feel too old to take on the responsibility of raising a family."

She took his hand. "Don't even think such gloomy thoughts. If God sends us children, we'll know how to take care of them."

"Then you will marry me, Norah? I love you."

A sweet song of delight filtered into the soft recesses of Norah's heart. "Yes, I will. You've said the magic words, *I love you.*"

"Then we'll be married as soon as I can stand unassisted before a preacher on my own legs."

"According to the doctor, that should be less than a month. I'll be ready."

Norah found the thought very satisfying. It seemed as if she'd started on the last lap of a long expedition when she'd come to the Sand Hills almost six months ago. Her journey had commenced when she'd responded to God's call as a teenager. Now twenty-five years later, as Mason drew her into his strong, protective embrace, she had reached the end of that trip, with another, more exciting journey beckoning.

Nestling in the warmth of Mason's embrace, Norah experienced the conviction that she was in the center of God's will. Lifting her face for his kiss, her heart whispered, "'I am the Lord your God, who teaches you what is best for you, who directs you in the way you should go.' God knows best what is best for me."

Epilogue

Twenty-five years later

Family members crowded the auditorium to celebrate the graduation exercises of their loved ones.

Norah and Mason watched in pride as their firstborn, Anna Marie, named for Mason's mother, walked to the platform to receive her diploma. Excitement mounted at the climax of the day's program, when several members of the seminary board presided over a commissioning service for three of the graduates.

When Anna Marie walked forward as one of the participants, Mason took Norah's hand, lifted it to his lips and kissed her trembling fingers. Before the prayer of commitment was made by the president of the seminary, Anna Marie said, ''With your permission, Sir, I'd like to have my mother, Norah King, stand by my side. Because I'm living the dream she had before I was born. She's never admitted it, but I believe she prayed that God would set me apart for His service. When I leave next week for Africa, I'm not going only as an ambassador for Christ, but I'll represent my mother, too.''

Norah's eyes were misty, but she was also proud as she stood beside her beloved daughter. Anna Marie knelt with the other two students, and as Norah placed her hand on her daughter's head, she surveyed the family who'd gathered to share this blessed moment in her life. All of her siblings, and many of their descendants, were in the audience. Her twenty-two-year-old son, Chris, and his fiancée, sat beside Mason.

The years she and Mason had shared flashed through Norah's mind. They'd been very good years! Her association with H & H had been a true missionary endeavor. After Anna Marie was born, Norah had limited her role in the program, but she and Mason had continued to provide the ranch and the horses. Eventually the program had become so successful that H & H bought the Bar 8 to use as a year-round therapeutic facility for handicapped people of all ages.

Although Mason had doubted his ability to be a

good parent, he needn't have worried. It was almost as if he'd regained his youth when he became a father. He'd given the kids guidance in preparing their 4-H projects. He'd never missed a ball game when either of the children played. And he'd provided for them financially by purchasing large insurance policies that matured when Anna Marie and Chris were ready for college. Although he'd nearly driven Norah to distraction during the final months of each pregnancy, fearing that she wouldn't survive, he spent every minute in the delivery room with her. He suffered every pain she experienced and was there to rejoice when she gave birth to their daughter and son.

Ah, Mason, she thought, *how God has blessed us!* For not only had He sent them a daughter with a missionary zeal equal to Norah's, but Mason had heirs for the ranch. Intercepting her glance, Mason mouthed, "I love you," and the song that had its beginning in Norah's heart the first time she'd met Mason exploded into a mighty crescendo.

*　*　*　*　*

Dear Reader,

In *Song of Her Heart*, the heroine couldn't determine how God wanted her to fulfill her teenage vow to become a missionary. After a lot of soul-searching throughout the book, she finally learns that if she puts her trust in God and follows His leadership, she'll be in the right place at the right time to witness for Him.

I'm starting this letter at the beginning of the year 2002, having great expectations of what God will do through me in the coming year. But also looking backward to the year 2001, when my husband and I had the opportunity to witness our faith under circumstances that we could never have envisioned.

For over a year, we had been scheduled for a two-week tour of Ireland September 6-20, 2001. The tour started off on a happy note, as we took advantage of a long layover at Kennedy International Airport to go into Manhattan for a visit and lunch with some of the Steeple Hill editors. As we drove into the city by taxi on September 6, we enjoyed the view of the skyline, noting especially the Twin Towers, never dreaming that on our return from Ireland, they would be gone.

We were eating lunch in an Irish pub in Glengarrif when a waitress told us what was happening in New York. The fourteen of us on the tour were devastated at being away from home when tragedy struck, yet we bonded together with our Irish guide and bus driver in a way that would not have been possible under normal circumstances.

To observe the nationwide three minutes of silence on the day of mourning declared by the Irish government, our group gathered on a cliff overlooking the Bay of Dingle. After the period of silence, oral prayer was offered, and then we sang "America" and "God Bless America." There wasn't a dry eye among us. Our personal faith and our belief in the omnipresence and goodness of God not only sustained us during that tragic time, but seemed also to be a blessing to our group members. We were in the right place at the right time.

If you'd like to contact me, my mailing address is P.O. Box 2770, Southside, WV 25187.

Irene B. Brand